"Just What Do You Think You're Doing?"

Christa couldn't move.

"Well! Are you deaf as well as dumb?"

With this she turned to face Paul Talbot. He was taller than she remembered, and at that moment it was a considerable disadvantage.

"I'm Christa Emery, and I have every right to be here!"

"Of the Emery School of Music, isn't it? Is it morbid professional curiosity to see the 'fallen genius' that brings you here, Ms. Emery?"

Before she knew what was happening, Paul thrust his paralyzed left hand in front of her face. "All right—then look! Maybe you'd like my autograph, too? Fortunately, I'm right-handed."

But Christa couldn't possibly look. Tears blinded her as she ran to escape his rage.

MAGGI CHARLES

is a confirmed traveler who readily admits that "people and places fascinate me." A prolific author, Ms. Charles states that if she hadn't become a writer she would have been a musician, having studied the piano and harp. A native New Yorker, she is the mother of two sons and currently resides in Massachusetts, with her husband.

Dear Reader:

Silhouette Romances is an exciting new publishing venture. We will be presenting the very finest writers of contemporary romantic fiction as well as outstanding new talent in this field. It is our hope that our stories, our heroes and our heroines will give you, the reader, all you want from romantic fiction.

Also, *you* play an important part in our future plans for Silhouette Romances. We welcome any suggestions or comments on our books and I invite you to write to us at the address below.

So, enjoy this book and all the wonderful romances from Silhouette. They're for *you!*

Karen Solem
Editor-in-Chief
Silhouette Books
P.O. Box 769
New York, N.Y. 10019

MAGGI CHARLES
Magic Crescendo

Silhouette Romance
Published by Silhouette Books New York
America's Publisher of Contemporary Romance

SILHOUETTE BOOKS, a Simon & Schuster Division of
GULF & WESTERN CORPORATION
1230 Avenue of the Americas, New York, N.Y. 10020

ISBN: 0-671-57134-6

First Silhouette Books printing February, 1982

10 9 8 7 6 5 4 3 2 1

For my cousin, Kay . . . with love and the echo of so many beautiful musical memories.

Chapter One

It began raining as the bus crossed through the Berkshire Mountains, and the driver was forced to slow down. Christa, peering out at the passing countryside, felt anxious about making her connection. By the time they reached Albany, the rain was slashing angrily against the windows. At the depot, there wasn't even time for a quick cup of hot coffee. Christa dashed through the downpour, catching the Lakeport bus just as it was about to pull out. Taking a deep breath, she squeezed down the narrow aisle and sank into a rear seat, her clothes nearly as damp as her spirits.

On the long drive up the Northway, the rain intensified, blocking out potential views of the gorgeous, peak-season autumn foliage. Christa closed her tired eyes and, forced to look inward, began concentrating on her own thoughts.

They were a strange melange. She had not been in Lakeport for over three years, nor would she be returning now except for the fact that her Uncle Julian had suffered a heart attack, and had asked for her.

Julian Forsythe. He was her uncle by marriage only, having been married to her beloved Aunt Faith, who had taken Christa into her home after her parents were killed in a boating accident on Lake Champlain, this when she was not quite twelve.

"Home" had become the Emery School of Music, which had been founded many years before by Christa's grandfather. The Emerys had always been a musical family and Faith Emery had been the last of the line, an excellent musician herself, an even more wonderful teacher. Many of her pupils had gone on to brilliant careers, the most famous of them being the internationally renowned concert pianist, Paul Talbot.

Even as she thought of Paul, Christa shivered slightly. She had seen him in concert in Boston the previous spring and he had been sensational, returning to center stage time and time again to accept the tumultuous applause that was so rightfully his. Watching him from the audience, it was difficult to believe that this magnificent figure, impeccable in white tie and tails, his black hair gleaming like satin and a purely incredible smile etching his strong features, was the same person who had come to study with Aunt Faith during the first couple of summers Christa lived in the old music school.

Paul was already a student at Juilliard then, Christa remembered, but he still had returned to Aunt Faith for instruction during his vacations. He must have had a great deal of confidence in her!

As for Christa, during those first years of her teens she had been secretly, hopelessly, in love with him. Although he had not yet developed the mature, virile fullness that had been so evident at the concert last year, he had been a very handsome young man. Also, he had been outgoing; there had been nothing stuffily temperamental about Paul Talbot.

Christa remembered a Saturday afternoon when, after a lesson, he had, on the spur of the moment, asked her to go to the movies with him. Later she had not been able to recall a thing about the movie, for she had, even then, been overwhelmingly aware of Paul's physical nearness. They had eaten popcorn together, and to Christa that popcorn had had an almost celestial quality. . . .

At the concert last spring, she had been tempted to go backstage and introduce herself, but she had hesitated. She read every word she could find about Paul, and there was quite a bit printed about him in newspapers and magazines; he was the sort of artist who captured public fancy, with that mixture of tremendous talent and astonishing good looks. Thus she knew that he recently had become engaged to a New York socialite named Gloria De Platte. This meant that Miss De Platte undoubtedly would be backstage, and even though Christa was sure Paul would have welcomed her, once she had "identified" herself, she shrank from the thought of seeing him with the charming and beautiful young woman whose picture frequently appeared with his on the society pages.

So, when the concert was over, she had quietly merged with the crowd filing out onto Huntington Avenue, and returned to the Brighton flat she shared with a friend who worked in the same office with her.

Yes . . . thinking of Lakeport brought forth a strange mixture of memories, she conceded now, as she stared through the blinding rain. Aunt Faith had died three years ago, when Christa was eighteen. Uncle Julian had closed down the music school, but he had continued to stay on in the rambling old house the school had occupied, and had built up a good trade as a piano tuner.

Christa had stayed with him, through the summer after her graduation from high school. She knew that her aunt had wanted her to go on to a conservatory of music for further study. Aunt Faith had felt she had an excellent chance of making a success as a concert pianist, and she had imagined that this wish, on her aunt's part, must have been communicated to Julian before Faith died.

If so, however, he shortly made it clear that he had no intention of honoring it. He said frankly that he would not help Christa with the financing of a musical education, because ever since he had married into the Emery family he had seen for himself that music, at best, was a precarious career. Christa, he had pointed out, with a certain callousness, was essentially alone in the world, and also penniless. He favored her doing something practical, something that would ensure her earning a living.

She had been crushed, but she also had been entirely too proud to let Julian Forsythe know how she felt about his edict. Also, the fact of the matter was that she had very little choice in regard to her future course of action. He was right. She *was* alone in the world, and she had no money.

It was bitter to accept his loan of sufficient funds to see her through secretarial school in Albany and, since graduating and getting a job in Boston, she had regularly remitted ten dollars to Julian out of each week's pay, this toward discharging her debt to him.

It was at school in Albany that she had met Glenda Murray, a bubbling redhead who was as outgoing and expansive as slender, blond Christa was shy. Glenda's father was a lawyer in Albany, and it was through connections of his that word came of two openings in a Boston law firm. She had prevailed upon Christa to go to Boston with her, and they had been living together for over two years now.

Christa had been more than happy to make the move. She had needed to get Lakeport out of her system, in effect to wash the Emery School of Music and all the memories it held out of her life, so taking the Boston job had been a good choice. She and Glenda got on admirably, even though she sometimes annoyed her roommate by refusing to double date, saying that she'd much rather stay home with a good book.

She hadn't realized the reason behind this until last year, when she had seen Paul Talbot in that concert appearance. Then it had come to her, forcefully, that quite inadvertently she had been comparing everyone she met with Paul all these years, and no one, thus far, had measured up to him, and, after seeing him in concert, she wondered how anyone ever possibly could.

But the lingering vision of him standing on the stage, gracefully receiving a standing ovation, also left in its wake the realization that she and Paul had taken such different paths they might as well be living on separate planets. Thereafter, she had chided herself bitterly though subconsciously, and she made a sincere effort to join in on parties with Glenda and her friends, but the effort had been exactly that—more effort than pleasure.

Despite herself, despite the full realization that Paul Talbot was completely out of her orbit, she could not shake the long instilled habit of scanning newspapers and magazines for news about him. The latest she had read was that he was doing a spectacularly successful concert tour of Latin American capitals, having started well south of the equator during the past summer, which, she realized, would have been winter in those regions.

At least he would not be in Lakeport, she told herself, which, for the sake of her own peace of mind was just as well!

Christa already had determined to stay in Lakeport only as long as her uncle needed her, and she was still surprised to think that he actually had sent for her in his illness. They had never been close, and his decision about her musical education had left a decided chasm.

Yet, she realized, Julian had no other family, and

neither did she. They were both alone, both of them, though in differing ways, the last of their lines.

Christa had brought only one suitcase with her. Now, at the Lakeport bus depot, she stashed it in a storage locker, deciding that she would go to the hospital and check on Uncle Julian before thinking about where to spend the night.

She found a taxi to drive her to Champlain Hospital, and realized, with a faint smile, that it was the first time she had ever used a taxi in Lakeport. Growing up here, she had walked everywhere she went for the most part until, reluctantly, Uncle Julian had given her driving lessons, this at Aunt Faith's insistence, and so she had gotten a license.

She had never had a car of her own, however, nor was Julian generous with his venerable Buick, which must be close to a classic by now.

As she settled in the corner of the taxi, the rain having penetrated through her raincoat clear to the fabric of her tailored brown suit, Christa wondered if she should, perhaps, have taken her suitcase directly to the old music school on Birch Street. She still had a key to the house, so entry would present no problem, and she could have checked to be sure the furnace was on, and could also have switched on a couple of lamps. As it was, she would be returning alone after dark, if she decided to stay at the music school, and she didn't relish the thought. It might be better to see if the Lakeport Inn had a vacancy.

At the hospital, the taxi pulled up to a sweeping entrance that surprised her. They had been building an addition when she left town, she remembered now, and it obviously had been completed and was surprisingly modern, the walls in the spacious reception lobby done in oyster gray, with contemporary furniture in tones of purple, fuchsia and light blue.

Not all that long ago, Christa had recognized most

of the people she saw around town but the taxi driver had been a stranger, and the receptionist at the desk was a stranger too. She was a chic young brunette with an automatic smile, but when Christa gave her name, the smiled dimmed, just momentarily, leaving Christa with an odd sense of disquiet. Then it came to full voltage again and the girl said, "Take a seat, won't you, Miss Emery? Dr. Baldwin wants to speak to you. I'll page him."

The day, the rain, the memories, had all taken a toll. Christa crossed the lobby feeling weary and depressed as she sank into a light blue chair.

Almost immediately, a tall woman who had been sitting nearby stood, and came over to her.

"Christa!" she said. "You *are* Christa Emery?"

Christa looked up into a face made especially compassionate by large, expressive, hazel eyes. Even though hair that once had been raven black had turned to white, it was a face that still would be instantly recognizable to anyone who ever had been seriously interested in the musical world.

Honora Talbot. Paul Talbot's aunt. Honora Talbot *Brent,* Christa corrected silently. The famous soprano, now a widow, had been happily married to her manager for many years.

Honora Brent had been a close friend of Aunt Faith's, and Christa had heard the story many times of how Honora had first brought Paul to take lessons from Faith when he was just a little boy. There had been something special about his talent even then, something that these two gifted women had recognized and nurtured.

Christa stood up quickly, and although she was of average height herself, Honora Brent was considerably taller. She started to speak, but she was stopped by the expression on the older woman's face. She tried to define it precisely, and a single word came to mind.

Sympathy.

At once, she felt herself flooded by a swift sense of apprehension. She said, stammering slightly over the words, "Yes, I'm Christa Emery. And—you're Mrs. Brent, aren't you?"

"Yes," Honora Brent nodded. "Christa, I . . ."

She was interrupted by the appearance of a tall, gray-haired man, wearing a doctor's white coat.

His glance swept from one woman to the other, then he said to Christa, "You must be Miss Emery."

"Yes. I am."

"I'm so very sorry, Miss Emery. . . ."

"Dr. Baldwin," Honora Brent interposed, "I haven't had the chance to tell her."

The doctor frowned. "Miss Emery," he said, tight-lipped but clearly trying to be as gentle as possible about it, "your uncle died two hours ago."

It was a shock.

Christa had never *loved* Julain Forsythe, but somehow this didn't lessen the initial impact of the doctor's announcement.

Uncle Julian was *dead;* now she would never know why he had sent for her, what it was that he must have wanted to tell her.

She reminded herself that she had come as quickly as possible. The message from Champlain Hospital had reached her at her office, her employers had been extremely solicitous, not even letting her linger to finish up some typing she was doing but passing the letters along to Glenda. She had gone back to her apartment, hastily packed her suitcase, and had taken the first bus out of Boston that would lead to Albany, and thence to Lakeport.

Could she have flown? Economy, she admitted, had been a consideration in taking the taking a bus rather than a plane, but the way the weather had turned out there was also a strong chance that planes at Logan Airport would have been grounded by the time she got there, and she had no idea what possible connections might have been available from Albany to Lakeport.

Still, she could have found out, and if there had been a connecting flight, she might have gotten here in time. She told herself this bitterly, and then the fact of death, forever overwhelming, seemed to swamp her, and she stared at Honora Brent and the doctor with desperation in her lovely blue eyes.

Honora grasped her arm firmly. "Look," she said, "we're going into the cafeteria and get you a cup of strong, hot tea, laced with plenty of sugar."

The doctor nodded approval. "I'll check on you both in a few minutes," he promised.

Christa, feeling totally numb, allowed Honora to virtually lead her down corridors and into a spacious dining room. She dutifully waited at the table Honora chose, while the older woman crossed to the cafeteria line, and bought the tea.

It was scalding, and much sweeter than she normally liked tea, but she drank it obediently under Honora's watchful eye, and it did seem to have a restorative effect.

Finally she felt as if she could focus again, and the first thing of which she became conscious was the concern etched on Honora Brent's lovely face.

"We tried to reach you in Boston but you had already left," Honora said, her voice low toned and beautifully musical. "I spoke with a friend of yours. Glenda?"

"Glenda Murray, yes. We share an apartment."

"We thought of asking the police to intercept your bus, but Dr. Baldwin and I both felt it would be a terrible jolt to you. Christa, I'm so *sorry*. . . ."

Despite herself, despite trying to hold back tears, Christa's eyes misted.

Honora Brent reached out and took her hand.

The older woman's hand was slim and strong, and she wore a glorious square-cut emerald, surrounded with diamonds, on her fourth finger.

She said, "We felt, darling, that it was better to let you get here and then tell you. There was simply no way of avoiding this being a ghastly experience for you. You *did* bring luggage with you, didn't you?"

Christa nodded dully. "I put my suitcase in a locker at the bus station."

Mrs. Brent considered this, then came to a decision. "Fitch can get it later," she said. "I think it would be best if he takes us home first."

"Fitch?"

"Fitch and his wife Martha run my household for me. I don't know how I could possibly get along without them. They've spoiled me completely."

Christa found her voice. "Mrs. Brent," she said, "there is no reason why you should feel obliged to take me home with you. In the taxi on the way over here I decided to get a room at the Lakeport Inn, once I—checked on Uncle Julian's condition," her voice faltered as she said this. She got a grip on herself and continued steadily, "I also could go to the Birch Street house, for that matter. I have a key."

"It would be frigid," Honora Brent said. "You know your Uncle Julian. I'm sure he made certain the rescue people put the thermostat at the lowest possible level as they were carrying him out of the house." She said this matter-of-factly, quite without censure. "But regardless of that, I couldn't possibly permit such a thing, Christa. Tomorrow will be time enough to look into the Birch Street house—and a good many other matters that you will be faced with. I'm sure when Dr. Baldwin joins us he will agree with my prescription for you, which is a hot bath, dinner in bed and a good night's sleep made possible by the sedative I'm sure he is going to prescribe for you, all this in a place where you will be with someone who cares for you."

Christa could not repress her start of surprise, and Honora Brent was quick to note it.

She said, the lovely musical voice saddened now, "You seem to forget, child, that your Aunt Faith was my dearest friend. We went to school here in Lakeport. Later, she stayed with her family while I went away into what I suppose might be called another world, but we never lost track of each other. Then, while I was still quite young, my husband and I were given the care of my nephew Paul, and this is something we were both grateful for as we never had any children of our own. We raised Paul with your Aunt Faith's help, I might say. His parents had been killed tragically too, just as yours were, but this was when he was only three years old. Unfortunately, he doesn't even remember them.

"It is to Faith that credit must be given for sensing that Paul possessed a musical gift well out of the ordinary. I think she sensed the same sort of thing in *you*, Christa, but that is another story entirely, and we won't go into it now.

"What we *must* make clear is that I would feel as if I were making a farce of Faith's memory if I didn't persuade you to come home with me now, and her memory is very, very dear to me."

Honora released Christa's hand, and the emerald gleamed as she did so.

"Here's Doctor Baldwin," she said.

Chapter Two

During the early morning hours the rain ended, and Christa awakened to bright sunlight—a new day, a new world.

Last night, in many ways, was now a blur. The doctor had thoroughly endorsed Honora's "prescription" and Christa, weary beyond words, was led out to a big black car waiting at the curb, where Honora introduced her to Fitch, a wiry man with thinning gray hair and a pleasant, crinkly face, who wore a dark business suit rather than conventional chauffeur's livery.

Christa was conscious of the fact that her clothes were still damp, as she settled into the thickly upholstered back seat of the car with Honora, but she was much too tired to care, nor did the Talbot mansion, which had dazzled her so when she was younger, make any impression at all, just now. Inside, Martha, who was plump and gray-haired and had cheeks the color of cherries, prepared a hot, pine-scented bubble bath for her, and, as she lingered in it, Christa felt as if she were drowning in a wonderfully fragrant woodland.

Martha brought a tray to her bedside, wisely limiting the choice of food to an excellent soup, toast and hot cocoa. Honora came in to administer the sedative, and lingered until she was quite certain Christa was on the verge of sleep. Then she bent and

18

kissed her, and Christa felt enveloped in a kind of warmth she had not known since her Aunt Faith died.

Now she got out of bed and went to the window, and gasped at the absolute glory of the view that stretched before her. The Talbot-Brent mansion was directly on the lakefront, a few miles out of town. Christa remembered how she had always been struck by its beauty when she had come here with her Aunt Faith, but then these impressions had been overshadowed by the ever present hope that Paul Talbot would happen to come in while she was there.

She wondered where he was now. Buenos Aires? Lima? Rio de Janeiro? Or had he, perhaps, gone from South America to Europe on tour? Was he, even now, in London or Paris or Rome? Or was he possibly back in New York, preparing for a fall concert with the Philharmonic?

She also wondered if the full-sized concert grand she remembered so vividly was still the focal point in the lavishly decorated drawing room downstairs, and briefly she wished, wistfully, that everyone would leave the house so, if it *were* there, she could go and run her fingers over the keys. It was so long since she had played! She knew she must be hopelessly rusty, and could not face the thought of playing at this point in front of anyone—most especially Paul Talbot's aunt!

Thinking of Paul, the view from her windows became momentarily eclipsed, but now she centered upon it again, and it was pure visual delight. An expanse of lawn, green even now in October, swept from the house to the lakefront, terminating in a small and rather pebbly beach. Champlain itself stretched beyond, an inland sea studded by small, rocky islands crowned with spiky pines. Towering above the distant shoreline, Vermont's Green Mountains, punctuating the cloudless sky, were clad in all the magnificent tones of orange and gold and amber and crimson that blended together on nature's autumn palette.

The lake itself was a deep sapphire, a jewel among jewels. Champlain had always had a powerful impact upon Christa, fortunately not ruined by the fact that ten years ago it had claimed her parents' lives.

Her father had been a violinist and a good one, even though the right opportunities never really had come his way, or perhaps, she realized now that she was older, he had never tried to seize them or, more importantly, even recognized them for what they were. He was a dreamer of a man, and had his wife been more practical, their fortunes as a family might have been different. But Christa's mother had been a poet who published now and then in various literary quarterlies that paid little or nothing, and she really had wanted no more than this, in the way of a career, plus her husband and her small daughter.

They had been dreamers, all of them, Christa thought now, with slight bitterness. It ran in the family. No wonder practical Uncle Julian had, at times, been condemnatory of the Emerys and their ways.

Uncle Julian. Dimly, Christa remembered Honora Brent saying something last night about matters which must be attended to and, of course, there were.

Slipping on her dressing gown, she followed the beautifully curving staircase she remembered so well to a foyer on the lower floor that was decorated in tones of light green, gold and ivory. Beyond, she knew, was the drawing room, where the gold and ivory colors were picked up and enhanced by the rich brocaded drapes that framed the windows that looked out over the lake.

Now she peeked to see if the grand piano was still in its corner, and it was! Even this glimpse of it made her heart give an odd little thump.

The breakfast room, just off the kitchen, was furnished in maple, with yellow and white the main colors, spiced with touches of blue for accent. Honora, seated at an oval table, had been reading a newspaper, Christa saw, and she took off the glasses she used for such purposes and flashed a welcoming smile.

Christa sat down near her hostess, and accepted the glass of orange juice Martha brought her. "I've always loved this house," she said, "but I'd be hopelessly spoiled if I lingered here very long."

"Would there be anything so wrong about that?" Honora queried.

"I'm afraid there would be," Christa said, between sips of the juice. "I've a job in Boston, and I'm going to have to get back to it—and reality—as soon as possible."

Honora smiled tolerantly. "You seem almost afraid that you're in danger of straying," she pointed out.

"Not really," Christa said, then hesitated. "You were wonderful last night, Mrs. Brent," she said then, "but I do realize I—well, I've got to get a grip on myself."

"In other words," Honora said, with keen perception, "you feel this isn't your world, so you don't want to become too enmeshed in it, is that right?"

Christa's smile was wry. "That's very right," she admitted.

"Christa . . ." now it was Honora Brent's turn to hesitate. "Do you like your Boston job that much?"

"Good Heavens, no!" Christa blurted, before she could stop herself. "That is—it's just a job. Oh, the lawyers Glenda and I work for are very nice, they never quibble about our taking time off if we need to, and the pay is reasonably good. But . . ."

"It isn't a career?"

Christa thought of the grand piano in the drawing

room and bit her lip, hoping her feelings didn't show. "No." she said slowly. "No, it isn't a career."

"Then would you consider giving up the job if you could help me by doing so?" Mrs. Brent questioned.

"If *I* could help *you?*" The mere thought seemed ludicrous.

"Yes. To backtrack a bit, I took the liberty a little while ago of calling the funeral home, Christa. I had the chance to talk to your uncle before he died, and he told me what his wishes were. There is to be a very simple church service, with burial next to his wife in the Emery lot, if you have no objection."

"If *I* have no objection?"

"Well, it *is* the Emery family lot," Mrs. Brent pointed out. She hesitated. "Your Uncle Julian didn't have many friends, Christa," she said then. "In fact, it was Faith who was always the popular one. After she died, Julian became more and more of a recluse.

"He was not a man anyone—with the exception of Faith—could reach easily," Honora Brent continued. "I'll admit I often wondered what it was Faith saw in him, but love has strange ways—and wears many faces. Faith *did* love Julian—and he loved her. When she died, all the light went out of his life. I suppose what I'm trying to say is that I don't think there will be many people attending his funeral, and since he had no family there will be no one coming from a distance. So, with your permission, I've set the service for ten o'clock tomorrow morning."

Christa closed her eyes, and opened them to find Honora regarding her anxiously. She said quickly, "You don't need my permission. I—I appreciate your doing this more than I can say. I was dreading it."

"Very well, then. Tomorrow afternoon, I would suggest we have a conference with Julian's lawyer. Before he died, Julian told me—and I think this is what he wanted to tell you—that he has felt guilty, for a long while, because he made you give up a musical career. He thought, many times, about offering to send you to a conservatory after all, but it wasn't that easy. He really had very little cash to spare, though he made a reasonably good living tuning pianos, and his own wants were simple. Actually, he put a good part of his money into keeping up the old Birch Street house, and I give him credit for that. Last year, for instance, a new roof was needed, which cost him quite a bit. It's such a rambling old place, though, it still needs painting and a lot of other attention. I might add that there are many valuable antiques that belonged to your family, Christa, and would bring you quite a bit of cash on today's market if you choose to sell them. I can't imagine what the house itself would bring. In a sense, it's a white elephant, unless you became lucky enough to find someone who is looking for such a place. Then you might get quite a good price for it.

"Julian left enough money to bury him, and there may be a little cash aside from that; it won't be enough, though, I'm afraid, for you to keep up the house and the taxes should you not wish to sell. . . ."

Reality. It was facing her right here in Honora Brent's lovely breakfast room, and Christa swallowed hard.

"It's foolish, I know. I can't help but be sentimental about the music school—and yet I know you're right. I know it had become a white elephant even before Aunt Faith died, but it has been in the family so long. It's difficult to think of turning it over to strangers."

"Of course it is," Honora agreed. "That's exactly why I don't think it would be wise for you to make any quick decisions."

"I'm going to *have* to make quick decisions, Mrs. Brent," Christa said reluctantly. "As you've said, I can't afford to keep the place up, I have no reserves.

I've been trying to pay Uncle Julian back the money he spent sending me to secretarial school. I couldn't send him much, just a little each week, because it costs a fantastic amount to live in a city like Boston, even though Glenda and I certainly don't live very lavishly."

"I realize that," Honora Brent said gently. "That's why I asked you about your job. I had intended to wait a while before getting into this with you, but I see now that you're going to feel you must take the first bus out of Lakeport once you even begin to straighten things out tomorrow."

"That's true. I imagine I can deal with Uncle Julian's lawyer about everything by phone or letter, once we've met and had an initial discussion."

"That's probably so—but, regardless, I'm asking you to stay here, Christa."

Christa's smile was sad, her blue eyes cloudy. "How could I possibly?" she asked simply. "I would have to take total advantage of your hospitality, Mrs. Brent, and I simply couldn't."

"Believe me, I realize that! I also wish you could bring yourself to call me Honora. My nephew Paul calls me Honora."

At the sound of his name Christa felt herself flinching, and she hoped that this very astute woman by her side was not aware of her reaction.

Fortunately Honora, for the moment, was preoccupied with other things. She said, "I asked you if you would consider giving up your job if you could help me by doing so. I'm going to formalize that request now, Christa. I very much *need* help, and I'm offering you a job. I've been asked to write the story of my life, and I need someone to work with me on it. I think you must realize as much as I do that you would be the perfect person!"

Honora Brent was right. Very few people came to Julian Forsythe's funeral. Later, Fitch drove Honora and Christa to the lawyer's office on Court Street, and Christa discovered that Honora had been right again. Julian had left very little cash; this, however, plus the old music school and all its furnishings now belonged to Christa.

After leaving the lawyer's office, they drove to Birch Street, and as she tried to put the key in the lock on the old front door, Christa's fingers fumbled so badly that Fitch took it away from her and opened the door himself.

Even though Julian had had a new roof put on the year before, there were still water stains on the ceilings in the upstairs rooms where the old roof had leaked. Most of the rooms evidently had been closed off for months, and were now pervaded with an unpleasant, musty odor, plus a thick coating of dust and galaxies of cobwebs that sparkled when the afternoon sun brushed them.

Julian obviously had lived entirely in a small section downstairs, and he had not been a good housekeeper. Also, he had been stricken suddenly and had been in the hospital less than a week. There was still food in the refrigerator, the odor of sour milk assailing Christa's nostrils when she opened the door.

She could not resist running her fingers over the piano in the front parlor, which had been Aunt Faith's "teaching room." It was in tune. This, at least, Julian had attended to.

Aside from that, however, Christa was dismayed at the dilapidated condition of the old house. It didn't take a real estate agent to make her realize that, as it now stood, it would command a very indifferent sale price.

As she, Honora and Fitch drove back to the Talbot mansion, the sun was sinking behind the Adirondacks to the west, leaving a trailing veil of amethyst and rose shadows that swept across the lake, changing the sapphire water to indigo.

Martha had lit a fire in the family room, which was beyond the drawing room. This was a more intimate setting, the room furnished with comfortable chintz-covered couches and chairs, the bookcases lining the walls laden with a veritable treasure trove of reading material, interspersed with interesting bric-a-brac.

Although the family room could be approached via a side corridor, Honora and Christa walked through the drawing room tonight to reach it, and Christa was, again, painfully conscious of the grand piano, which evoked dual memories of her own music and Paul Talbot. To add to what was a near physical ache, she noted a framed portrait of Paul on the mantelpiece over the blazing fire. He was about ten years older than she was, she knew, which would make him close to thirty-two. This must have been taken three or four years ago, she imagined. In it, he looked somewhat younger than he had when she had seen him in concert last year, but every bit as handsome.

Honora, following her glance, asked suddenly, "You remember Paul, don't you?"

Christa could feel her throat constrict; she forced out the words, "Yes, of course."

Honora frowned. "It's quite a while since I've heard from him," she confessed. "He gave a concert in Rio several weeks ago, and I thought by now he'd be calling me from New York. The Rio concert was the last in the South American series." She shrugged. "I imagine Paul decided to take some time off before he starts the New York season, but even so—he's usually pretty good about keeping in touch."

Fitch's appearance with a decanter of sherry and two stemmed crystal wine glasses on a silver tray prevented Christa from answering, and for this she was grateful. She knew that in any discussion concerning Paul she was bound to become hopelessly tongue-tied, this very definitely a hangover from her adolescence. Honora, she could imagine, would be much amused to discover that, long ago, her best friend's niece had had a rather fantastic crush on her devastatingly attractive nephew; a crush from which, if the truth were to be told, Christa had never fully recovered.

Musing on this and trying to force herself *not* to look at Paul Talbot's picture, she recognized again, as she had on the bus coming to Lakeport, the possibility that the reason she had never fallen in love was very probably because of Paul Talbot, and she found herself resenting this.

She had been such an absolute fool all these years! If anything were needed to convince her fully of this it was living, for even this brief time, in Paul Talbot's home. It demonstrated, with supreme clarity, how far apart they were.

Honora's words cut through her thoughts. "I won't insult you by offering the going rate," she said lightly, handing Christa a glass of tawny-colored sherry. "I can see, though, that you're a long way away from me."

Christa very nearly said, "Not as far as you'd think"—biting back the words just in time as she quickly took a sip of sherry.

Honora tasted her own sherry, then she said slowly, "I wish I didn't have to rush this with you, Christa. But have you given any thought to my suggestion that you work with me as my assistant?"

Christa's blue eyes met Honora's hazel ones levelly. She said, "Frankly, no. I don't *want* to give your suggestion any consideration, Mrs. Brent—I mean Honora—because if I did it would become so terribly tempting!"

"And you don't want to face up to that kind of temptation?"

Christa shook her head. "I can't *afford* to face up to that kind of temptation."

"You think I'm doing this as a favor to you?"

"Yes, I do."

"Christa, I don't know how to convince you otherwise!" Honora stared at her wine glass. She said softly, "In many ways, I'm a lonely woman. I have friends here in Lakeport, of course, I could go an endless round, socially, if I wished to, but that no longer has much appeal to me. Occasionally I like to entertain people who really mean something to me. When Paul is in New York, especially, I love to go to his concerts now and then. As you can imagine, I'm tremendously proud of him. But he has his own life, his own career, he comes here very seldom. Most of the time, I'm by myself. I know it must sound tremendously maudlin to put it this way, but the fact is I spend hours living with my memories."

Honora had changed to a jade green caftan upon their return to the house. Now she shifted her position on the couch she was sitting on, curling her feet up under her like a young girl.

She said, "One day it occurred to me I actually do have a real story to tell. I've lived quite a life, Christa."

Christa smiled. "I *know* that," she said. "Aunt Faith used to talk about you all the time."

Honora nodded. "Well," she said, "Faith was the first to tell me that I should write my story. Life has taken me so many places, I've had so many fabulous experiences, met so many fascinating and famous people. . . ."

Honora stared into the flames, as if evoking visions. Then she said simply, "The thing is that in order to get this all down, I must have someone to tell it to. I can't do it alone, can you understand that? Further, that person must be absolutely *right.* I think I knew even before I spoke to you in the hospital that you were going to be the right one for me, Christa. I might add that I've already been offered a contract by a major publisher for my book, and it has become something I want so very much to do, for Paul and for your Aunt Faith, as well. I would surely dedicate it to her memory. But I need *you*. . . ."

Honora flung out her arms in a gesture that would have been overly dramatic had it been made by anyone else. "Can you understand that?" she asked Christa.

It took discussion, it took planning, and a certain amount of conciliation on both sides, but in the end they came to an agreement that caused Honora to call for Fitch to bring them a bottle of champagne, and she invited Fitch and Martha to join in a toast to her new alliance with Faith Emery's niece.

For her part, Christa insisted that if she became Honora's secretary-assistant in the writing of the book she would not live at the lakefront house. Rather, she would move into her *own* house on Birch Street.

Honora was going to pay her a salary that she felt was excessive, but it would, nevertheless, enable her to begin fixing the old place up. In her hours away from her work with Honora, she could do quite a bit of the necessary scrubbing and painting and polishing herself. In fact, the challenge of making something beautiful out of the old music school began to grow on her, and when Honora agreed to go along with her in regard to the living arrangements—for, at first, she was horrified at the thought of Christa living by herself in the Birch Street house—they were at the edge of final accord.

The weekend came, and Christa spent Saturday and Sunday, with Fitch's help—for Honora insisted on this, at least—cleaning and arranging a bedroom for herself, and converting Aunt Faith's "teaching room" into a living area. The kitchen was obsolete but the various appliances *did* work, and for the moment that was all that mattered.

Further, Christa discovered that with the house

and its contents she had also inherited her Uncle Julian's venerable Buick; the very same car in which she had learned to drive! Although close to ancient, it would give her transportation to such essential places as supermarkets, plus to her job at the Talbot mansion. She called Boston and explained why she must resign, and was assured by one of the partners in the law firm that if she wished to return at any time, there would be a job waiting for her.

She talked to Glenda, who assured her that she could get a sublet on the apartment they shared without any trouble, much as she hated giving up her favorite roommate. Further, Glenda insisted that it would also be no trouble to pack up and send along the rest of Christa's clothes, and other personal possessions. They had rented the apartment furnished.

Finally on Sunday night, after Fitch left, she sat down at the familiar old piano upon which Aunt Faith had taught her her first chords, and she began to play. Amazingly, her secretarial work, which had involved a great deal of typing, had served to keep up her finger dexterity surprisingly well.

Playing again was such pure joy that she nearly forgot about getting any supper for herself.

Monday morning she presented herself at the Talbot mansion at exactly nine o'clock and found that Honora was in the breakfast room, and insisted that they share coffee and brioche before they started the day's work. This proved to be their pattern, but, despite the fact that Honora was an extremely casual employer, they made progress as the days passed, and the story that began to emerge was even more fascinating than Christa had imagined it would be.

Halloween came, and Christa was delighted when a procession of trick-or-treaters rang her doorbell during the course of the evening. She had bought candies and apples, just in case, remembering as she did so how, in earlier years, Uncle Julian had discouraged such frivolities. But evidently the neighborhood youngsters realized there had been quite a change at the old music school, and Christa was pleased that they were not afraid to approach her, as they well might have been in view of Julian's austere reputation.

She went to bed Halloween night happier than she had been for a long time—only to face a first of November on which her entire world was to change, literally and totally, for all time.

Chapter Three

As she drove out to Honora's house on that morning of November first, Christa was full of tales of small witches and ghosts and pirates and demons that she was sure would delight her employer. She was in high spirits as she opened the front door, that morning after Halloween, and swiftly made her way to the breakfast room.

She stopped short when she saw that Honora was not waiting for her at the table, and suddenly she sensed that there was a kind of stillness about the place, almost a pall.

Frowning, she started for the kitchen, to meet Martha just emerging. There was no doubt about it; placid, cheerful Martha had been crying! Her eyes were red rimmed, and she was still wiping at them with the edge of her apron.

Something had happened to Honora! With the thought came fear, a many-tentacled kind of fear that wrapped itself about Christa so tightly that she could only stand rooted to the spot, staring at the housekeeper.

The words came in a whisper. "What's happened?"

Martha's tears surfaced again, and she choked out the words, "It's Paul."

Christa went cold.

Martha said, brokenly, "Go up to her, Christa, please. She just got the phone call about half an hour ago, she was still in bed. I was up in her room when the phone rang, and she got so white I was afraid she'd pass out on me. . . ."

Christa didn't wait to hear any more. She sped up the stairs and into Honora's beautiful bedroom which, like the bedroom she had stayed in herself when she first came to the house, faced out over the lake.

This was a cold and gray day, though. Champlain gleamed dull iron and menacing, and now most of the leaves had gone from the trees and the mountains across the lake loomed huge and barren.

Honora's room was decorated in glorious tones of peach and apricot and palest gold, but even these vibrant colors seemed to have lost their vitality today, reflecting the ashy-faced woman who lay, propped up by pillows, looking twenty years older than she had yesterday.

"Honora," Christa began. "Martha told me . . ."

Their eyes locked, and Honora saw, in Christa's, a terrible kind of finality, and she said, almost gently, "He isn't dead, dear—though maybe it might be better for him, in a way, if he were. The reason I haven't heard from him all this time is that he was in an accident in Brazil. He's been in a clinic—a world-famous place in Rio—where they've done everything possible for him, except the thing that matters most. His left hand is partially paralyzed, and there is no doubt that the paralysis is permanent."

Christa sank down on the edge of the bed, overcome. There were no words.

After a moment, Honora continued. "I haven't spoken to Paul directly," she said, speaking with obvious effort. "It was Ted Bentley who called, he is Paul's manager, and a good friend as well. He traveled with him throughout the South American tour, he goes on all the tours, for that matter. Often Ted goes ahead to the next city to make the necessary arrangements. . . ."

Honora's beautiful hazel eyes were shadowed, her mouth etched in misery. "I keep speaking in the present tense," she said, "but that's all over now."

It was with difficulty that Christa found her own voice. "When did this—this accident happen?" she asked.

"Several weeks ago. He had played the Rio concert and then gone to the *finca* of some friends to relax. It was on the return trip to Rio that they crashed, evidently rounding a curve on a remote mountain road, according to Ted. Ted had rented the car during their stay in Brazil, there were just the two of them in it. Paul was driving; Ted was thrown clear, and injured only slightly. For that matter, it seemed at first as if they had both escaped really serious injury. The car was 'totalled,' as Ted puts it, and initially they felt they had been very lucky. It was several hours, however, before they were discovered. This was just before dawn, when a farmer came by on his way to market in a town a few miles away. The man spoke no English, they spoke practically no Portuguese, but he assessed the situation and took them, in his wagon, into a small clinic in the town."

Honora sighed, and looked so pale that Christa asked, anxiously, "Can't I get you something?"

"You might ask Martha to make another pot of coffee and bring it up," Honora said. "I think we could use a jolt of brandy in it too, early in the morning though this is. You look as wretched as I feel!"

Christa, on her way to the bedroom door to call Martha, paused. "I saw Paul in concert in Boston last year," she said slowly.

"You've never mentioned that!"

"Well, I didn't see him *personally*." Christa amended hastily. "I thought about going backstage, but it had been so many years . . ."

"Paul would have been delighted to see you—if you had identified yourself—you *have* grown up over those years."

When Martha came with the coffee, Honora directed that a full measure of brandy be poured into each cup, and Christa sipped hers gratefully; at the moment, it *was* a restorative.

She asked, almost timidly, "Where is your nephew now?"

"Paul and Ted are in New York. They came in late at night on a flight from Brazil, they wished to slip back into the country as inconspicuously as possible. Because the accident did occur in such a remote place, Paul was not recognized. Later, Ted contacted friends in Rio, and they arranged for his transfer to a major clinic under an assumed name. Paul is quite dark, as you know, he could easily pass as a Latin. Also, he does speak Spanish, and so he was incognito, in the clinic, under a Spanish name. I might add that he comes by this legitimately. My mother had Spanish blood, I inherited her hair. It was raven black, when I was younger. . . ."

"I remember," Christa said.

"Maybe you remember too, then, that in the summer, when he had a good tan, Paul looked almost like a gypsy."

Christa could not quite echo that opinion, for in her memory Paul loomed primarily as the handsomest man she had ever seen, and he had *been* a man, even when she was on the threshold of adolescence. She had known him during the time when she was twelve to fourteen, and he twenty-two, or thereabouts, to twenty-four. Despite his kindness to her, and that unforgettable afternoon at the movies when they had shared popcorn, the ten year difference in their ages had, at that time in their lives, almost put them into different generations.

She said now, hesitating over her choice of words, "When was the decision made about his hand?"

"First, in Rio," said Honora. "They told Paul that had he been able to receive medical care faster, there might have been hope of restoring the life to his fingers. As it is, precious time passed before he was finally taken by the farmer to the small clinic in the little town where, Ted says, they were remarkably efficient, but they did not have the facilities for the kind of intricate, immediate neurosurgery Paul would have required. By the time he was transferred to the clinic in Rio, the damage was irreversible. They have been in New York for two weeks. Remarkably, Paul has still managed to remain incognito; except, of course, for the physicians who attended him first in Rio and then in New York, and they have guarded his secret. He maintains an apartment on Central Park West, within walking distance of Lincoln Center. Ted decided, however, that they would avoid the apartment for the moment, and so checked both them in under assumed names at a small hotel near Gramercy Park. The medical information was transmitted from Rio directly to the specialists in New York, even prior to Paul's arrival. Now a thoroughgoing study of the situation has been made, and the original opinion stands."

Honora's voice broke. "He is only thirty-two," she said. "He was barely approaching the peak of his musical potential—and now it is all over."

Christa finished the brandied coffee, and put down her cup. "Did he *refuse* to speak to you himself?" she ventured.

"He was still asleep," Honora said. "They've been giving him sedatives, I suppose, at least I should think so. That's why Ted called here so early, it wasn't much after eight o'clock. Paul has been putting off calling me from day to day. He persuaded Ted to wait until the specialists in New York had reached their own conclusions. Although, from what Ted tells me, they both had every confidence in the Brazilian doctors, there was still that slight thread of hope to cling to. Naturally, I can't help but wish that I had been notified immediately, but I can understand Paul's reluctance."

"And now?" Christa asked.

"Ted feels that it would be extremely traumatic for Paul to have to face the media right now, to stand up to interviews and all the rest. He says Paul desperately needs time in which to make an adjustment. They can't hope to stay around New York much longer without Paul being recognized; it's something of a miracle that he hasn't been already. Finally, last night, Ted had a long talk with him, and Paul agreed to his plan."

Christa could feel the hairs on the back of her neck prickling, and she sensed what the answer was going to be even before she posed the question.

"What plan?" she asked Honora.

"They are going to come here," Honora said simply.

The seconds ticked into minutes and the minutes into hours, and gradually the day passed. But Christa's own mental chaos seemed to increase rather than lessen, and by early afternoon she was exhausted.

It had been an impossible day, insofar as work was concerned. Honora was understandably not up to concentration; they flitted from one thing to another. After lunch Honora decided to try to nap, and told Christa that she might as well do the same thing since they surely were not about to accomplish getting down any worthwhile material until Honora, at least, had glued her own "pieces together again," as she put it.

Christa opted to return to the music school, rather than take advantage of Honora's offer of an afternoon nap in one of the guest rooms, plus an informal dinner together in front of the family room fireplace. There was always something in the way of physical work to be done in the old Birch Street house, and this, she knew, was what she needed as an outlet.

She drove home slowly, deeply immersed in her thoughts. It was dark and raw, the trees, so newly divested of their bright leaves, seemed especially stark. Christa shivered as she let herself into the house, and although she usually was extremely cautious about her use of oil, in view of the cost of heating, she thrust the thermostat up and got a fire going in the studio-living room that had for so many years been Aunt Faith's teaching room.

As the flames crackled, she found her eyes straying to the old piano upon which Paul Talbot had taken his first lessons. Its solidity, and the very fact that the notes were still there and as playable as when he had first touched them, seemed to her almost a reproach. She, certainly, had never felt less like playing herself, and whereas she normally left the keys exposed, now in a sudden, abrupt movement, she pulled out the covering case as if this simple gesture might shut out dreams and memories.

She realized now that for a long time she had been living vicariously, through Paul Talbot's career, insofar as music was concerned. She had not only read but had clipped every word she could find written about him; she had a box full of these clippings upstairs in her bedroom.

She had become especially devoted to this project after her Uncle Julian had put the finale to her own hopes of becoming a concert pianist. Then, it seemed almost as if Paul were playing for her, as well as for himself.

She acknowledged, now, that this had been a childishly romantic concept on her part; still, as she stood in the center of the room, the stillness, despite the sound of the crackling logs, seemed acute. It was a musical stillness that she was feeling, she realized. It was as if music had suddenly been swept out of the world.

Christa felt as if she were drowning in a peculiar kind of sorrow that had an edge of intensity to it such as she had never experienced before. She forced herself to set about polishing the furniture in the old dining room with a vigor that made it gleam as it had not gleamed in years, but work, she found, did not in the least alter this sorrow she felt for Paul Talbot; she ached for him.

When she finally realized that she was hungry, Christa opened a can of soup and heated it, then put it on a tray with a few crackers, and ate her impromptu supper in front of the studio fireplace, visualizing, as she did so, Honora very probably eating *her* dinner by herself in front of the fireplace in the lakefront mansion's family room.

It had been selfish, in a way, not to have stayed to dinner with Honora tonight. Yet, the need to be alone had seemed almost imperative, and she knew that the need to think things out *was* imperative.

If Paul was coming home, Honora would obviously want to devote her primary attention to him. It seemed most unlikely that she would give thought to resuming her life story until Paul had made the adjustment of which his manager had spoken—if, indeed, such an adjustment ever really could be made.

Then, there was also the realization that, to Paul Talbot, she, Christa, would be a reminder of her Aunt Faith, the woman who had started him on the path to his musical career, and she could well imagine that this was probably the last thing in the world he would wish to be reminded of just now.

She would be a thorn of sorts to Paul, she felt sure of this. But even more relevant was the fact that if

Honora were to put aside her book, the services of a secretary-assistant would no longer be needed.

Christa sighed, and watched the fire die out, the glowing embers fading to dull grayness. She really had just begun to get her stride, both in the job with Honora, which had completely immersed her, and in a plan to gradually put the music school back into order. There had been the added pleasure of playing the beautiful concert grand in the lakefront mansion, as well as practicing here in the studio for sometimes two or three hours before she went to bed at night.

There really would be no room for a piano in an apartment such as the one she and Glenda shared in Boston, which meant that, once again, it was going to become necessary to thrust music out of her life, to say nothing of leaving this place that, even though dilapidated, was beloved to her, and of giving up what had become a very wonderful relationship with Honora. In this short time she had become devoted to the former diva, and even Martha and Fitch seemed almost like members of her family. . . .

Through the evening she pondered about these things, even though she knew, reluctantly, that there was only one logical conclusion.

In the morning she would have to tell Honora Brent that she was leaving.

Chapter Four

It had rained during the night, the tree branches, caught by the wind, brushing against Christa's windows like unwelcome, skeletal intruders.

She arose to face a day even grayer than yesterday had been, and saw that the rain had turned to sleet.

She had already resolved to get to the Brent house earlier than usual, for there had been some correspondence to attend to yesterday that she had frankly forgotten. This was, in part, because she and Honora had been using two work areas. When Honora was "talking" her story, they usually stayed upstairs, in a luxurious boudoir-study off Honora's bedroom, the walls lined with autographed photos of the world's most famous operatic, musical and theatrical stars. It was an ideal setting for the project they were involved in.

When attending to more mundane details, however, such as writing letters of request for information or answering some of Honora's surprisingly voluminous correspondence, Christa worked in a library that was directly across the entrance foyer from the drawing room. Now she resolved that she would secrete herself in there this morning and finish up the small pile of odds and ends that had accumulated while, hopefully, Honora still slept. Then she would have to face up to telling her employer-friend that she felt it imperative to leave before Paul returned home.

The lakefront road was slippery, and Christa nearly went into a skid as she turned into the driveway that led to the house. She continued the rest of the way with especial care. All Honora would need at this point, she told herself wryly, was another accident.

She parked at the side of the house, intending to go in via the kitchen door in the hope that Martha would have a pot of coffee perking, but a glance toward the kitchen windows revealed that the lights were not yet on as they surely would be, on a day like this, if Martha and Fitch were up and working.

She really *was* early. She glanced at her watch and saw that it was not yet seven-thirty.

Turning her collar up and pulling her rainhat down firmly, thankful that she had coiled her long, ash-blond hair into a twist today or it would surely have gotten soaking wet, she walked close to the house, barely skirting the plantings and almost slipping on the sleek, semi-frozen grass, until she reached the front door.

Once inside, she went directly to the library as she had planned, spreading her raincoat and hat over a chair to dry, and then slipping out of her shoes, which were sodden.

She stood, barefoot, pondering for just a moment. The house was warm, but there was a fire laid on the hearth, and she decided she would light it. The library was almost medieval in design and furnishings, with leaded glass windows and heavy oak furniture. Normally, with the rows and rows of books with their fine leather bindings reflecting jewel-toned colors, Christa considered it one of the most beautiful rooms in the house, but today, like everywhere else, it seemed dismal.

The brief walk around the house had chilled her thoroughly, though, and she decided that before lighting the fire she would go out to the kitchen and make coffee herself, if Martha or Fitch hadn't come down in the interim.

Her bare feet traversed the beautiful Oriental rugs in the foyer, and she felt warmed, briefly, by the deep pile of the lush gold carpeting in the drawing room, then as she was about to continue toward the kitchen she was arrested by the sight of the great concert grand in the corner, which, today, had a poignantly special significance.

If a piano could be said to be in mourning, this piano was surely in mourning.

She approached it tentatively, standing before it, touching a key with a slender finger but not pressing it. Musical sounds carried, especially to another musician, and she had no wish to awaken Honora prematurely. But even as she was about to turn away, a voice, lashing out at her from the vicinity of the family room door, had the effect of welding her to the spot where she stood.

"Just what the hell do you think you're doing?" the voice demanded angrily.

Christa literally could not move, for what seemed like a fair sample of eternity. She did not have to be told who this was. She *knew*.

But her moment of seeming eternity could not have been all that long for he said now, impatiently and with considerable disgust in his tone, "Well! Are you deaf as well as dumb?"

With this she turned to face him, slowly, reluctantly, her eyes drawn. as if by a magnetic force, to a pair of gray eyes that rivaled in tone the weather outside and were considerably more threatening.

She had not realized how tall he was; this was her first impression of him after she found the strength to draw a quick breath that emerged as an audible gasp. She was slightly above medium height herself, but he towered over her, and at the moment this was a considerable disadvantage.

He looked down at her with a disdain that made her flinch. He certainly did not remember her; that was painfully apparent. If, once, he had taken a slim, blond teenager to a movie and bought her a bag of popcorn, that incident had been inextricably erased from his mind and, Christa realized, she could have hardly expected it to be otherwise.

He continued to glare at her, while she desperately tried to find her own voice, which was eluding her, when she needed it the most, as it never had before.

She sensed that he was furious, absolutely *furious*. His eyes narrowed; they seemed almost metallic as he surveyed her and had she not known who he was she would have been terrified. Even *knowing* who he was, it was difficult not to be afraid of him, and she shrank back inadvertently.

Why should he be so angry? This was the single thought of which she seemed to be capable right now. She could understand surprise, shock, displeasure even, at coming upon her like this, and she thanked heaven that she had considered the hour and thus hadn't yielded to the temptation of sitting down and playing something on *his* piano one last time. But he must have realized that she had access to the house, or did she look like some sort of thief to him? Did he think she had come to steal, to vandalize—what *did* he think?

As she began to recover both her breath and her composure, questions of her own came to Christa. What was he *doing* here? Did Honora know that he had arrived? Certainly when they had been talking yesterday Honora had no idea that he was coming on from New York almost immediately!

He was watching her closely, but there was no lessening of anger, of antagonism; she could feel them sweeping over her like a great, crashing wave, frothing around her, becoming ever deeper.

"Who *are* you?" he asked, snarling the words.

Her surname stuck in her throat. Emery. The

Emery School of Music. Her Aunt Faith. The associ-
ation, she was certain, would come to him all at
once, and she wasn't sure that either of them was
ready for it! So she said, lamely, the words seeming
distressingly timid, "I'm your aunt's secretary."

"Secretary!" Each letter of the word dripped
scorn. "My aunt has no secretary. Who do you
represent? What paper? Or is it a radio station? Or
do you have a whole damned TV crew waiting up the
driveway?"

So that was it! He thought that she represented
the media, he thought that his privacy was about to
be invaded, he thought that she . . .

Despite herself, her mouth twitched into the semblance of a smile, and it did not go unnoticed.

"Just what is so damned funny?" he asked her
icily.

"You think I'm some sort of a reporter," she told
him. "But honestly, Mr. Talbot, I *am* your aunt's
secretary. At least—I have been. I intend to give
notice today, but I came here early to attend to some
paper work we didn't manage to cover yesterday. I
felt rather chilled when I got here, though, and I was
on my way out to the kitchen to make coffee. . . ."

Now that she had found her voice the words began
to tumble one over the other, and this only seemed
to irritate Paul Talbot further.

"It seemed to me," he said very coldly, "that you
were about to sit down and play the piano."

She could feel her heart thump at the mere
mention of the word piano, and it was all she could
do not to glance at his left hand. As it was, now that
she had found breath and voice again her other
senses were recovering as well, and she was finding it
disconcertingly disturbing to be so close to him.

He was wearing an ivory-colored Irish-knit sweater that emphasized the darkness of his hair and the
powerful, muscular build of his chest and shoulders.
His long legs, equally muscular, were sheathed in

perfectly fitting dark blue corduroy slacks. He seemed pale; this, Christa realized, was due to the fact that he had so recently spent weeks in the hospital; but the lightness of his skin only heightened the steel gray coldness of his eyes. They were icy eyes, she decided. She wondered if they could ever possibly be really warm?

He had shaved this morning, early though it was, and she could smell the faint, rather spicy tang of the lotion he used. There were shadows under his eyes and he looked tired, yet there was also a surprising aura of vitality about him—or was it virility, Christa wondered, uncomfortably, or maybe both?—in view of the experience he had just been through.

She would have expected him to be depressed, morose, withdrawn. She would have understood it if he refused to speak to anyone at all. But she most definitely had not been prepared for this tall, disturbingly handsome stranger—for *this* Paul Talbot definitely was a stranger to her—who had unhesitatingly blasted her and now was still waiting for her answer to his assumption that she had been about to play the piano.

She said, swallowing hard, "It's a bit early for music, don't you think?" and then was appalled at herself for touching upon the subject of music at all with him.

However, he merely shrugged. "Possibly. I suppose it's a matter of opinion," he said, then added, "do you always come to work barefoot?"

She had forgotten that she had left her wet shoes in the library, and she said, discomfited, "No, I . . ."

"I don't need to hear an explanation. I was just curious about whether it's customary these days for *secretaries* to go barefoot." He emphasized the word secretary, making her realize that he still disbelieved her, and now her own anger was piqued.

She said stiffly, "I don't want to go upstairs and

awaken your Aunt Honora just to verify my creden-
tials. But when she *does* wake up, I can assure you
that she'll substantiate the fact that I work for her. A
New York publisher has given her a contract to write
the story of her life, and I have been acting as her
secretary-assistant."

"For how long?" he demanded suspiciously.

Christa held her chin high. "For the past three
weeks."

He laughed shortly. "How far have you gotten?
To the middle of page one?"

She turned away from him, refusing to dignify this
with answer, and he said abruptly, "Just a minute,
Miss—you do have a name, don't you?"

She faced him defiantly. "Yes," she said, her voice
as cold as his. "My name is Christa Emery."

Something flickered in the gray eyes, and she held
her breath. Then he said levelly, "The Emery
School of Music. That's it, isn't it?"

"Yes."

"You must be Faith Emery's niece. Is that why
you sneaked in here with this silly story about
working for my aunt? So that you could see the
damaged goods at first hand? Morbid professional
curiosity, shall we say?"

Before she knew what he was about to do he
thrust his left hand out, almost in front of her face
and said tautly, "All right, then, *look* at it! Maybe
when you're done you'd like my autograph. Fortunately, I'm right-handed."

Even had she wanted to look at his hand, Christa
could not possibly have done so, just then, because
her eyes had filled with scalding tears, tears of
outrage, humiliation, and a desperate kind of anger.

She said, chokingly, "That was *filthy* of you! What
do you think my Aunt Faith would say if she could
hear you?"

She did not wait for his answer. She turned and
ran blindly toward the kitchen, nearly bumping into

Martha who, having just arrived downstairs, had heard voices in the drawing room and started toward the door.

"Christa!" Martha exclaimed, then, seeing the cascading tears, added, "what has happened to you? You're not hurt?"

"No," Christa said, trying with all the force at her command to stop crying, but the tears continued to flow.

Martha thrust something in her hand, and she realized that it was a linen face towel. Clutching it, she sank down in a chair by the kitchen table, literally burying her face in the towel until the sobs diminished.

Martha, she saw as she lifted her head, was waiting, and she said placatingly, "Now, dear, can't you tell me what happened to upset you so?"

"I met the great virtuoso!" Christa said bitterly. "I could hardly sleep last night, literally aching for him, after Honora told me about his accident yesterday. But now, believe me, I don't care *what* happens to him. He's the most despicable person I've ever met in my life. Honora doesn't deserve to have a nephew like that!"

She should have sensed the warning in Martha's eyes, but she didn't. It was only when Martha said, helplessly, "Mr. Paul . . ." that she swung around to see Paul Talbot standing in the kitchen doorway staring at her, his face as white as the woodwork.

Before she could speak he turned on his heel, and a moment later she heard his footsteps receding up the front stairway.

She had botched it, she had botched it completely. Christa was only too well aware of this. No matter how she felt about Paul Talbot's initial confrontation with her, she should have taken his recent experience into consideration and certainly should not have said the things she had to Martha. Words once spoken, however, could not be obliterated, she mused, as she drove back to the house on Birch Street. Once again she tried to plunge herself into work on the house, as a kind of antidote, this time tackling the kitchen cabinets which needed a thorough cleaning out, first, and later a good paint job. She could find no panacea in physical work today, though, nor did she want to settle down with a book, as she might have done, usually, on a miserably sleety day such as this one, nor, certainly, did she want to touch the piano!

She knew that she should call the law firm in Boston, to see if there really *was* a job there for her now, and also she should find out whether or not Glenda had gotten another roommate and, if so, if she could possibly find a place, even if it were only a temporary furnished room, which Christa could move to as quickly as possible.

Just now, though, it was impossible to be coherent about any plans. The incident with Paul Talbot had been much too upsetting.

She continued to putter, to try to keep herself busy, but when, toward lunchtime, the doorbell rang, she was glad of the diversion.

Christa opened the door to a strange young man who smiled at her and said, "You *are* Christa Emery, aren't you?"

He had an especially open and friendly sort of smile, and his manner and appearance matched it. He was slightly taller than she was, well built, with sandy brown hair, light green eyes, and freckles, and all he needed, she decided, was a fishing pole in hand to make him seem like a perennial Tom Sawyer.

The car parked just behind hers at the curb, however, was a sleek silver Corvette, and the man himself who, she suspected, was probably about thirty, when one looked at him closely enough, despite the initial youthful impact, was dressed in

casual but expensively well-tailored tweeds with a
turtleneck pullover, over which he wore a light tan
raincoat.

The sleet had turned to rain again and he said,
"May I come in, Miss Emery? My raincoat's sup-
posed to be waterproof, but I'm not. I'm Ted
Bentley."

She stood aside to let him enter, the name not
registering immediately; then it came to her.

He was Paul Talbot's manager. He had been in
Brazil with Paul, he had, in fact, been involved in the
same accident. Realizing this, Christa wished briefly
that she had closed the door in his face, and her
expression showed it.

Ted Bently, watching her, said quickly, "Please.
Hear me out, will you?"

There were double doors with frosted glass panes
at the entrance to the music school, leading into a
vestibule centered by a hanging ceiling lamp with a
multi-colored Tiffany shade. Christa had turned on
the light before opening the door, in view of the
dreariness of the day, and although she didn't realize
it, the rainbow hues cast by the shade bathed her
blond hair in radiance, creating a halo effect that,
tired as she was, made her seem both fragile and
especially lovely.

Despite this seeming fragility, though, she was
again in control of herself; she'd had all morning to
get herself together after the initial outburst which
she so deeply regretted, and she was not about to
become embroiled again with either Paul Talbot or
his manager.

She said, civilly but coolly, "I doubt there is
anything to hear you out *about,* Mr. Bentley."

"I wouldn't say that," Ted Bentley said disarming-
ly, and Christa recognized a certain steel beneath his
casual exterior and began to appreciate why Paul
would have chosen someone like this to act as his

business manager. Charm, she was sure, was a commodity with which Bentley was well endowed, and she sensed that he was about to try a fair dosage of it on her now.

"I'm quite sure my employer didn't send you here to see me," she said emotionlessly, "so that means it must have been her nephew. In that case, we really *do* have nothing to say to each other."

Ted Bentley's green eyes, which were considerably sharper than they seemed at first, were surveying her deliberately.

He said directly, "I'm not speaking for Paul, if that's what you're inferring. Paul is quite capable of speaking for himself and, yes, I do have the impression that he wants to talk to you. Actually, however, I've come with an invitation from Mrs. Brent. She was going to telephone you, having received a message you left with Martha, but since I had to drive into town to the pharmacy to get a few things she suggested I stop by and ask if you'll come back and have lunch with us. She said that since this was originally supposed to be a workday she doubts you would have made any other plans."

He had her there! Christa gritted her teeth, then relaxed sufficiently to say politely, "I really would rather not. Would you tell Mrs. Brent that I'll telephone her this afternoon?"

"Mrs. Brent doesn't want to talk to you on the phone, she wants to talk to you face to face," Ted Bentley said. "Paul evidently told her you plan to hand in your resignation, and she's quite upset about it."

"She certainly must understand the reason for it."

"I'm not that well versed on the situation," Paul's manager said frankly. "If you don't mind, though, will you either come along with me or invite me to sit down somewhere? I was in the hospital for a time myself with a wrenched knee after the accident in

Brazil, and this kind of weather doesn't exactly make it pleasant to stand around, even with a beautiful young lady like yourself!"

The way he said this had a double effect on Christa. He was lightheartedly amusing in the way he paid a compliment but also, without censuring her, he had made her aware of her own temporary lack of manners insofar as being a hostess was concerned.

She said quickly, "Come into my studio, won't you?" and she noticed that he *did* limp slightly as he followed along by her side.

He had left his raincoat in the vestibule. Now he sat down in her favorite armchair and smiled up at her. "That's better," he admitted. "Now, *I* don't think you need to do anything to enhance your appearance, but *you* probably do, so why don't you run along and do whatever you think needs to be done so we can get on out to the house for lunch. I know that I'm starving, and I'll bet you've had next to nothing to eat today."

She hadn't, nor yesterday either. She shook her head at him and said, "Do you carry an invisible crystal ball? Really!"

"Yes, I know," he said blandly, "I'm impossible! Everyone tells me so, but sometimes my technique works."

Despite herself, she smiled back at him. "I'll just bet it does!" she agreed.

Once upstairs in her bedroom, she quickly changed from the old clothes she had put on to clean house to a blue mohair sweater and matching skirt. The color nearly matched her eyes, giving them an added emphasis, and now she combed her hair carefully, so that it swirled around her shoulders, and took more pains than usual with her makeup.

Ted was a skillful driver, but this was the kind of weather that demanded full time and attention to handling the wheel; they spoke very little on the way out to the lakefront mansion, and the closer they got to it the more Christa began to wish that she hadn't so easily given in to Honora's suggestion that she come for lunch.

Then it occurred to her that Paul probably would not even be present at lunch. Certainly he must have no more wish to see her again than she had to see him. Realizing this, she relaxed a bit.

Ted was right about one thing. It wouldn't do to merely offer her resignation to Honora over the telephone. This was something they must talk out, especially if—as Ted had indicated—Honora didn't understand the reason why she felt she must leave.

Yes, she decided, as Ted turned in at the driveway and drove the Corvette up to the front door of the house, she owed Honora a personal explanation, at the least. It was better this way. Much better.

Chapter Five

Because she had been so certain that Paul would take refuge in the sanctuary of his own quarters, Christa was completely dismayed when she walked into the family room with Ted to find both aunt and nephew sitting near the blazing fire sipping sherry.

Paul was wearing the same Irish-knit sweater and snug-fitting corduroy slacks in which he had appeared this morning, but his dark hair had been freshly combed. It was thick and smooth with just a hint of a wave.

Honora was wearing a deep coral velvet housecoat that emphasized her dramatic coloring; her eyes seemed darker than ever, her own arresting hair even whiter. There was a definite note of relief in her lovely voice when she saw Christa.

"My dear," she said, "I'm so very glad Ted persuaded you to come back with him."

She glanced at her nephew. "I understand you and Paul met earlier today."

Paul, who had stood as she entered, said, to her surprise, "Christa and I met years ago, Honora. I'll admit, though, that I didn't recognize her when I came upon her in the drawing room this morning." He actually smiled. "You've changed a bit, since you were twelve," he told her.

"Thank God for such blessings," said Ted, bridging the gap that threatened because Christa could, once again, find nothing at all to say, and realized that never before in her life had there been so many occasions occurring in quick succession during the course of which she had found herself virtually stripped of vocabulary.

"Sherry?" Ted asked.

"Yes, thank you," she said, and, taking the glass he handed her, chose the chair nearest Honora's.

She was acutely conscious of Paul's presence, and of the way he sat casually on a thick, green hassock, seemingly very much at ease. Glancing at him from beneath lowered lashes as she sipped her sherry, she found it very hard to relate *this* Paul to the imposing figure who had bowed again and again on the Boston concert stage last fall, except for the same disconcerting dark good looks; but even his attractiveness seemed double-faceted now.

Paul Talbot, as the artist, had been a "presence." She supposed she automatically had expected a certain carryover into Paul Talbot the man, yet here in his own home he projected an entirely different image.

This, common sense told her, was not all that unexpected. Professionals—especially actors, concert artists—often *did* project entirely different images, but the theory was that "offstage" they were, more often than not, not as attractive as they were before the floodlights, whether these floodlights were real or symbolic.

This, Christa realized, was not the case at all with Paul Talbot. Paul Talbot the man was every bit as devastating as Paul Talbot the artist. The thought came, unbidden, that to someone who really *knew* him, Paul Talbot the *man* might be the more devastating.

Also, she could not help but feel an admiration for him that was grudging, to an extent, because of the way he had behaved toward her initially this morning. He had been rude, extremely rude, and she had retaliated like an angered bee, struck to the stinging point. Nevertheless, he *had* to be admired, if only for the way he could come back to his childhood home and sit before the fireplace drinking sherry with an enviable aplomb, the only visible signs of the terrible tragedy that had befallen him so recently that slight pallor, and the shadows beneath his eyes.

Even as she conceded her admiration for him, for his courage at least, not realizing that she had, now, raised her lashes and was looking at him quite directly, he glanced toward her and their eyes meshed in a cataclysmic moment. In that instant, she knew that no matter how pleasant he might appear on the surface, even to remembering having met her all those years ago, he had not forgotten her speech to Martha in the kitchen, and she flushed.

"Christa, dear. You are so quiet," Honora said, as Ted refilled her sherry glass.

Fortunately Christa was spared an answer by Martha coming to the door to announce lunch, but as they went into the dining room Honora paused long enough to take her arm and say, "You and I must talk later, Christa. We'll go to my boudoir."

Surprisingly, Paul, coming up behind them, said, "I'd like to speak to Christa privately myself, after lunch, Honora."

Ted laughed. "How about letting me in on the act, too?" he complained whimsically. "I think there are a lot of things I could find to say to Christa. Shall we draw straws to see who goes first?"

Ted's banality carried the luncheon, actually, and he was the only one who did full justice to Martha's delicious cream of pumpkin soup, a light and fluffy cheese omelette, green beans in a savory herb sauce, and a coffee mousse for dessert that, Christa was sure, must contain a thousand calories per teaspoon, for it was so sinfully delicious.

Christa realized that Martha had tactfully chosen

dishes that did not require cutting, and she noted that Paul kept his left hand concealed beneath the table. He managed to do this so adroitly, however, that had she not known of his injury she would not even have noticed it. For that matter, she reminded herself, his left hand, supposedly, was only partially paralyzed, which meant that he might very well have some use of it.

As they left the table, Christa noted that the sun was trying to break through the clouds, casting weak yet definite rays of lemon light through the window-panes.

Paul, following her glance, said, "Do you think it would be too cold out for a stroll, Christa? I think if we followed the gravel paths down to the lakefront, it shouldn't be slippery."

She had not expected such an invitation, and before she could form a refusal Honora said quickly, "It would do you both good. Paul and Ted arrived quite late last night—without giving any notice, I might add," she said, shaking a finger at them, "or we would have stayed up to welcome them! As it was, we all got up and didn't get much sleep thereafter. You look as tired as we do, child. It will be chilly out, though. Paul, get one of my warm coats out of the closet for Christa."

Honora paused at the foot of the staircase. "Take your time, darling," she told Christa. "I shall probably nap for a bit. But come upstairs when you get back."

Honora made this last statement very positively, and Christa knew that there was no way she was going to avoid not only a complete explanation of why she felt she must leave her job, but probably some strong argument on Honora's part aimed toward prevailing upon her to stay.

Paul had gone to a closet off the foyer, and he came back wearing a thickly padded jacket of his own, and carrying a wool coat of a beautiful shade of sapphire that could have rivaled Lake Champlain itself on the sunniest of days.

He held it for her, using both hands without any apparent effort, and as she slipped into it his fingers lightly brushed her hair, accidentally, she was sure, since he certainly would not have done so on purpose. Still, she felt a kind of shiver at his mere touch that was quite unlike any sensation she had ever known before. She found that she wanted desperately to turn toward him, and it took all her willpower to say, "Thank you," and walk in the direction of the door instead.

The weather had warmed enough over the past couple of hours so that, as Paul had suspected, the gravel paths were not slippery, and they walked down the slope to the lakefront side by side, then began to pick their way along the pebbly beach.

Paul, glancing down, said, "I see you decided to wear shoes for this occasion."

Christa could feel the color surging into her cheeks. She was conscious of the beautiful Talbot mansion looming at the top of the rise above them, colonial in style, with lines that came close to architectural perfection. The house had been built with the magnificent lake view in mind; a majority of the principal windows on both the first and second floors faced toward the lake, and Christa was aware that Honora, or Ted, or Martha or Fitch, for that matter, could be watching them at the moment, and she wished that they could go farther away. It was almost as if the house had ears as well as potential eyes.

Paul seemed to sense her distress and he said, "Look, Christa, I was only teasing you. . . ."

"I know," she said. "I *know!*" She looked at him and said desperately, "Oh, blast it! I'm not going to cry again!"

He raised an ironic eyebrow. He said, "I seem to have that effect on you."

She noted that he had thrust his left hand into a pocket of the jacket he was wearing, but now, with his right hand, he removed a neatly folded white handkerchief from another pocket and handed it to her. "Just in case," he said.

"You don't have to be so sarcastic!"

"I wasn't trying to be sarcastic. I was merely trying to be helpful. If you're going to unleash the kind of flood you did this morning, my handkerchief will hardly be adequate, but at least it will serve as a start in the mopping up process."

She didn't answer him. She strode on ahead, until she had reached a small point that jutted out into the lake, and she rounded it, without even pausing to think that now the Talbot house *was* out of sight.

Her pulse was pounding, and she seethed with a mixture of embarrassment, antagonism, and various other emotions which she wasn't about to attempt to define at the moment; she only knew that Paul Talbot in the flesh affected her even more strongly than she might have suspected he would. Her feelings spun in a kind of swirl, and she marched faster as if to keep pace with them, forgetting the unevenness of the ground until her heel caught on a stone and she started to pitch forward.

Instantly she was caught and pulled back by a very strong right arm, nor was Paul content merely to pull her back. He also pulled her around so that she was forced to face him, and she saw, to her dismay, that anger etched his face again.

"Are you really *trying* to break your neck?" he demanded. "You asked me this morning what I thought your Aunt Faith would say if she could hear me. What do you think she would think about you? Because I questioned your appearance in my aunt's drawing room was there any reason for you to say the things to Martha about me that you did?"

"You *were* filthy," she reminded him, momentarily forgetting that actually she had planned to apologize to Martha for the things she had said as soon as the opportunity presented itself. "How could you think that anyone who had ever had anything to *do* with Aunt Faith, let alone her own niece, would sneak into your aunt's house to—to spy on you, as if you were some wounded creature in a zoo?"

He flinched, his lips tightening. He said, "You *do* have a way with words, don't you? But, do you know, that's precisely how I feel? I *feel* like some wounded creature in a zoo, or at least I feel that's the way it's going to be when all those people who used to come to applaud find out that I can't entertain them anymore. That's what I dread. *That's* why I was so furious when I thought, at first, that you were some snooping reporter who had found out about me despite Ted's precautions, and Ted *has* been astonishingly inventive. I should probably recommend him for a job in a top secret organization where they are thirsting for real ingenuity, now that I'll no longer need a manager."

There was a bleakness in the way he said those final words that summed it all up.

His career was finished. His need for Ted was over.

He seemed visibly to shake himself out of what Christa suspected must be a threatening mood of something close to despair, nor could she blame him if it was. He said, "Did you twist your foot, when you almost fell just now?"

"No."

He tried to smile. He said, "Good. I *think* I could carry you back to the house, but I can't be entirely positive. I'm somewhat below my normal strength quotient."

Then, sobering, he added, "I know I very definitely owe you an apology, Christa. I was rude to you this morning. Even if you *had* been a wayward girl reporter who had somehow gotten through my net, I would have had no right at all to speak to you like that. When you told me you were Faith Emery's niece, or I suppose I should say Faith Forsythe, it was unforgivable for me to say what I did to you, and to thrust my ugly hand right in your face as well. I suspect you know the truth, without my spelling it out for you, because I understand you're quite a musician yourself. I'm—very sensitive, about the hand. It's something that will take quite a bit of getting used to."

Was it something that he ever would be *able* to get used to? What did a man do when, not quite thirty-two and at the zenith of success, everything that meant anything to him was suddenly snatched away?

Paul was watching her intently. He said, "You have a very expressive face, and I imagine you are as perceptive as you are expressive. What are you thinking about me, Christa?"

She could feel that telltale rush of color flooding her cheeks again, but she knew that no matter how it might annoy him, this was a question she could not answer.

He continued to regard her, his gray eyes traveling from her hair, slightly blown now into a disarray that was far more becoming than she suspected, to her widely spaced, deep blue eyes, almost matching the coat she was wearing in their depth, and on to her slightly tilted nose, then down to her generously full lips. He had released her, after making sure that she was all right, but now suddenly his gray eyes seemed to acquire new depths, Christa had the feeling that they were twin mountain lakes which, seemingly bottomless, were unfathomable, and in which it would be singularly easy to drown.

In a quick gesture, he put *both* arms around her, pressing her so close to him that she was overwhelmingly aware of his taut, muscular strength and could hear the pounding of his heartbeat, even through the heavy jacket. His mouth made no preliminary searchings; the object of his quest was self-evident. His lips came down directly on hers, forcing her to part her own lips so that now there *was* a kind of exploration, and she clung to him, exquisite sensation following exquisite sensation.

Swiftly, using his good right hand, he unbuttoned her coat, then zipped open his own jacket, still holding her with his left arm, pressing her close to him so that she could feel the mohair sweater crushing against his chest.

Just as suddenly, a picture flashed, fully developed, into Christa's mind. Gloria De Platte! His fiancée! She could *see* the picture of the two of them in the paper, taken after the announcement of their engagement.

Christa pushed him away from her, with all the vigor she could muster, her cheeks flaming, but this time with indignation rather than passion. Or was it, she asked herself, if she were to be strictly honest about it, a combination of both?

She started to button the coat and he stepped back as if she had slapped him; as, in a sense, she had.

He was parchment white, a muscle in the side of his jaw twitching, and she knew that he, also, was angry; but this time she suspected that his anger was focused upon himself, rather than upon her.

"Christa . . ." he began.

But she stopped him. "Please," she said. "I don't want to hear anything you have to say!"

He stared at her. "In the name of God, why not?"

"Because this was wrong, completely wrong. There's nothing that can be said about it."

"Wrong?"

She had started back toward the house along the path, picking her way carefully this time. She had no desire to create another occasion in the course of which he might be required to take her into his arms.

He said, the words laden with heavy irony, "May I ask why you find a simple kiss between two adult human beings so *wrong*? Are you really *that* much of a child?"

A simple kiss between two adult human beings! Was *that* what he called it?

"Mr. Talbot," Christa began, but he interrupted her roughly.

"Must you be a complete imbecile?" he said irritably. "At the least, you can call me Paul!"

"All right then. Paul. I came for this walk with you because I wanted to tell you that despite your rudeness this morning . . ."

"I've apologized for my rudeness this morning."

"I realize that, and I've accepted your apology. But, as I was about to say, regardless of whether you had apologized to me or not, *I* wanted to apologize for the things I said to Martha. But that's the end to it."

"The end to *what*?"

"The end to anything either of us needs to say to the other."

They had reached the beginning of the gravel path that led up to the house, which was wide enough so that they could walk side by side.

He said, looking down at her with that quizzical lift to his eyebrow that she found so extremely disconcerting. "Perhaps you are not as perceptive as I gave you credit for being."

"Just what do you mean by that?"

"I don't think there's a need to explain at the moment, and even if there were, I am not about to," he said enigmatically. For a long moment, he was quiet, while her thoughts whirled. There was still Honora to face, and she knew that, for more reasons than ever, she must bring her employment here to an end.

He once again surprised her totally by asking quietly, "Where are you studying?"

"What do you mean?"

"Well, I presume you must be at some conservatory."

"What makes you presume that?"

He looked honestly surprised. "Your Aunt Faith had great confidence in your ability," he said. "She had as much faith in your potential, I'd say, as she did in mine, and that was considerable. You were still quite young last time I saw you, so, of course, I've never heard you play. Honora says you've been playing for her now and then, however, and she praises you very highly. I'd imagine this job was a sort of interim thing, between your regular studies. Am I wrong about that?"

"Completely wrong," Christa said stiffly.

They were abreast of a side path that led to a flight of steps which, in turn, gave entry to a back hallway in the house. Without waiting for him, Christa made the turn, ran up the steps, and was thankful to find the back door open.

She stood with her hand still on the inner knob, her back pressed hard against the paneling, for at least five minutes, before she managed to regain sufficient composure to take the next step, which, inevitably, meant confrontation with Honora.

Chapter Six

Honora was lying on a champagne velvet chaise lounge in her boudoir, thumbing through the current issue of a fashion magazine, but Christa was virtually certain that she had not been able to nap, and that she was not even looking at the pictures in the magazine, much less reading the text.

Perhaps it was a trick of lighting, for the sun had receded, November was once again staking a gray claim, but it seemed to Christa that Honora really *had* aged in the course of these past two days. The telephone call from Ted Bentley yesterday had taken an initial toll; keeping up the sort of brave front that she *must* have been keeping up since Paul's arrival had only added to it.

Yesterday! Could it possibly be only yesterday that the realization Paul was coming home under such terrible circumstances had come not only to Honora, but to herself as well? Was it only *this morning* that she and Paul had faced each other over the piano in the drawing room?

Honora said quietly, "You look exhausted, darling —and I know I am. Needless to say, I couldn't nap. And it doesn't seem as if the walk with Paul could have been very relaxing for you."

Relaxing! Christa remembered his arms about her, the pressure of his body, the searing touch of his lips, and she shuddered involuntarily. Paul Talbot had evoked in her feelings that she had never before sensed, even dimly. In fact it seemed to her now, in retrospect, she had, until this morning, been *incredibly* naive, a complete romanticist, living in a dream world where Paul Talbot, taking bows at center stage after a concert, was her equivalent of the proverbial knight in shining armor, and this concept was, in itself, a very tired cliché.

But, she thought dully, it might have been better to have left it at that. It might have been better, much better, if she had put the music school up for sale immediately after Uncle Julian's death and gone back to her job in Boston. True, when she accepted the position with Honora, she had had no thought that it would involve Paul in her life, on even the slightest level. Or was that really so? Had she hoped, via Honora, to be kept abreast, at least, of Paul's activities, to learn more about him, to come to know him vicariously?

What a stupid, infatuated little fool she had been!

She frowned, thinking about this, and Honora's eyes narrowed. "What has Paul done to you?" she asked abruptly.

Christa hadn't expected this sort of question; it flustered her, and she knew very well that Honora was much too sharp to miss this.

There was no point in simply stammering out, "Nothing," which was about the most she was capable of at the moment. Instead, fighting a surge of emotions, she walked across to the window and stared out at the lakefront where, just a short while ago, she had walked with Paul. She was conscious of Honora's eyes on her back, and finally Honora said, impatiently, "Christa. Come over here and sit down, will you please?"

For no logical reason, she felt like a chastised child. She chose a chair she had loved from the moment she walked into the boudoir, a small armchair done in a lovely, mauve-striped satin, and she sank into it.

Honora said, "If they hadn't arrived so late last night, I would have called and told you that Paul was here, Christa, so that you would at least have been forewarned. As it was, it was nearly midnight when they arrived. By the time we finally all got to bed, it must have been after two. I didn't even consider startling you out of your sleep at that hour, but now I almost wish I had."

She sighed. "Strangely," she said, "I think one of the worst problems is that Paul looks and seems so normal. He's rather pale, but that will change, of course, as he gets some rest and regains his full strength. There seems nothing wrong with him at all; even the scars on his hand are minimal, when one considers the terrible damage they caused, and they too will fade in time. He already has become adroit in almost camouflaging his bad hand, and he will become even more so. Even now, I think most people wouldn't notice his handicap unless they knew about it.

"No," Honora said, "it is the *invisible* scars which are so ghastly in Paul's case, and they are there, Christa. He is trying very hard to cope with this, it occurs to me that perhaps he is trying *too* hard. It's rather akin to not crying when someone you love deeply dies. It's much healthier to let grief out. I discovered that for myself when I lost my husband. . . ."

Honora paused, and Christa said, almost impatiently, "Honora, I know how this must be for him. At least, I can surely appreciate it. You don't have to convince me. . . ."

"I'm not trying to convince you of anything, child. I suppose I'm trying to assuage my own worry, because I *am* worried about Paul. Terribly worried. At this time in his life, he needs tremendous understanding. He has Ted behind him, of course. He has me. But . . ."

The question simply erupted. "What about Gloria De Platte?"

Honora's hazel eyes sharpened. "What about her?"

"I should think that she would be the one to . . ."

"To sustain Paul?" Honora queried. "I can't quite imagine Gloria in that role, Christa," she continued, her words laced with irony. "As a matter of fact, Ted tells me that Paul has not yet told her anything about the accident, or its results. Gloria went to Europe with her family while he was in South America. I believe at the moment she is holidaying somewhere on the Adriatic coast."

Christa frowned. "Certainly he'll have to tell her before much longer," she said. "Didn't you say he had a concert scheduled with the New York Philharmonic?"

"Among other concerts, yes. Ted had an extremely busy season booked for him. All of these appearances will have to be canceled, of course, and Ted realizes that the moment is at hand, whether or not Paul is ready to face up to it. He plans to go to New York the first of the week and issue a statement. We talked about that this morning, before I asked Ted to stop by at the music school. When the press release is issued, there will *really* be clamoring for interviews, and all the rest of it. Paul, we both feel, *isn't* ready for that. He needs time to get his life into perspective—which, God knows, is going to be a very heavy job for him. . . ."

"Yes?"

"It is *very* important, just now, that we keep the fact of his being here a secret," Honora said. "Only Ted, Martha, Fitch and myself know about it—and you, my dear. Unless, that is, you've mentioned anything about Paul's returning home to anyone else, since yesterday."

She hadn't, of course. Yet, Christa realized, she easily could have. If she had placed the call to Glenda, she might very well have said something about Paul's tragedy. She doubted that she would have mentioned it to Mrs. Anderson, yet had her neighbor stopped by this morning instead of Ted Bentley, there was the chance that she quite innocently might have done so.

She said, "I'm glad you told me this, Honora. I really hadn't thought about keeping Paul's homecoming a secret. I suppose I imagined that by the time he came back to Lakeport any press releases that were to be issued would have been. Now, however . . ."

"Now you *do* see how important it is that we protect Paul until he is ready to face the world again?" Honora suggested. She frowned. "I dislike that word 'protect.' It connotes weakness, and Paul, definitely, is *not* a weak person. That's precisely why he does need help, or the offer of help, I might better say. It is something he never would ask for!"

No, Christa conceded to herself, remembering the anger in those gray eyes this morning, he certainly wouldn't.

Honora rearranged a pillow behind her back. Then she said, "Now that you understand the situation, Christa, we can get back to settling our own affairs. Yours and mine."

Christa's smile was wistful. "Honora," she said gently, "you know perfectly well that we don't have any affairs to settle. With your nephew here, you certainly are not going to be able to continue with your book, and that means that you have no further need for my services."

She continued, her voice trembling slightly, "It has been wonderful, being here with you, really wonderful."

Really wonderful. Yes, coming to the Talbot house each morning, working with Honora, sharing the recollections of her fantastically colorful life, had, indeed, been wonderful. But, in its way, it also had been devastating.

Although Christa had not thought about this consciously before, it came to her now that Honora Brent was a very wealthy woman. Some of her wealth had been inherited from her family, some of it had been made, under her husband's expert management, over the course of her career. The Talbots, though, Christa realized dully, had always been wealthy. Honora had inherited this house from her family, but one day it would doubtless become Paul's. And, the house itself was a reflection of the kind of life that had always been natural to both Honora and Paul. Each piece of furniture was exquisite in its own right. The rugs, the fabrics in each room had been chosen with a magnificent eye for color, and many of them were now heirlooms. Every vase, every painting, the many small *objets d'art*, every single thing, to the massive concert grand piano itself, bespoke background and taste and money.

Neither Honora nor Paul had ever known what it was like to scrimp until the next payday, as Christa had done more than once since going to work in Boston, or how it felt to lug heavy bags of groceries up three flights of stairs to a cramped and crowded apartment that was too hot in summer and too cold in winter.

The silence had been a long one. Christa was keenly conscious of Honora's eyes upon her, and finally Honora said gently, "All right, my dear. Out with it. Paul told me you intend to proffer your resignation, and I want to know why. He admitted he was horribly rude to you this morning, but do you think that justifies your thrusting *me* out of your life?"

Christa said miserably, "He thought at first that I was a reporter, Honora. He thought I'd somehow

sneaked in here. That's why he was so angry initially. Then, I was standing by *his* piano, I was touching
the keys. When he found out who I was, he thought I
was a macabre curiosity seeker. That—that made me
furious."

"As well it might," Honora nodded.

"Well," Christa said, swallowing hard, "he said
some rather terrible things to me and then he
overheard me say some really ghastly things about
him to Martha and—it was a bad time. But he has
apologized to me, I've apologized to him, and that
has nothing at all to do with why I'm leaving you."

There was a strange expression in Honora's eyes.
"You're quite certain of that?"

"Yes," Christa said. "All right," meeting the
older woman's eyes levelly, "I *do* find him disturbing. He is a very—difficult person. Also, he connects
me with music, in fact he thought I was a student at a
conservatory somewhere, and I think that is a connection he would prefer to do without, for the
moment.

"Anyway, as I've already said, now that he has
come back here to live you can't possibly expect to
continue with your book, so that automatically puts
me out of a job, don't you see? It isn't because I'm
unappreciative, Honora, it's because I *am* apprecia-
tive that I am giving you my resignation, if we must
put it that way."

"In other words," Honora said, "it's an absolute
necessity?"

"I would certainly say so."

"Then," the older woman suggested, almost lan-
guidly, "why don't we let Paul offer his opinion
too?"

Honora's eyes were fixed upon the doorway, and
Christa swiveled in her chair to see him leaning
against the doorjamb, his arms crossed.

He had changed the Irish sweater, and she had a
sudden suspicion that this was because she might

very well have gotten lipstick on the neck of its
cream-colored surface as he held her against him.
Now he was wearing a perfectly tailored gray wool
shirt that almost exactly matched the color of his
eyes. It fitted him snugly, emphasizing his broad
shoulders, and making her especially aware of his
really excellent physique.

How long had he been standing there? Had he
heard *everything* she had said to Honora?

He was not about to reveal it, if he had. His
expression was quite noncommittal. He crossed the
room and sat down on the end of his aunt's chaise
lounge, seeming somewhat larger than life and ex-
cessively masculine against the background of
champagne-colored velvet.

As he glanced across at Christa, his gray gaze was
cool; it seemed impossible that less than an hour
earlier she had been locked in his arms as he kissed
her with an intensity that literally had bruised her
lips.

"I'd welcome the chance to venture an opinion,"
he said, speaking without any particular emphasis.
"As Christa obviously has told you, Honora, we
both got off to a bad start. We also tried to make
amends—at least I did—but that didn't work out too
well either," he said deliberately.

"Nevertheless," he continued, only that ironic lift
of an eyebrow betraying the fact that he was not
quite as unruffled as he would have one believe, "I
can see no reason why she thinks she needs to give
up her position here because of me. As I understand
it, you've been offered a book contract for your life
story, in fact you've already signed one. Is that
right?"

"Yes, it is," Honora said quietly.

"Then," her nephew told her, "I think I should
offer my congratulations. I've heard enough of your
story myself over the years so that I feel it would
make a terrific book, and you certainly should write

it. If I felt that *I* were going to block you from doing so, I surely wouldn't stay here."

"That's ridiculous, Paul, and you know it," his aunt told him.

"I hope so," he said, surveying Christa coolly, "but our Miss Emery seems to think otherwise. I hope you can convince her she is wrong, since it appears that the two of you work exceptionally well together, from what you tell me."

He rose, and stretched. Outwardly, at least, he was very much the dominating male, totally self-assured, in perfect control of himself.

He said, with no change of tone or expression, "Perhaps it will be an incentive if I assure your Miss Emery that I will stay out of her way during her hours here with you, Honora, since I seem to be her stumbling block. I've no wish to interfere, nor interest in interfering, I can assure you."

With that, he bent and brushed Honora's forehead with a light kiss, and without another glance in Christa's direction left the room.

Once again, a routine was established. Each morning at approximately nine o'clock, Christa arrived at the lakefront house and joined Honora in the breakfast room for coffee. Paul was never present on these occasions.

Ted Bentley went to New York, staying at the Central Park West apartment as he issued his press release and then met with members of the media in a series of sessions. There was an old black and white television set at the music school that Christa seldom turned on, but when she learned from Honora one day that Ted would be appearing on major TV that night to talk about Paul, she could not refrain from curling up in front of it, and later wished she hadn't.

As a part of the interview with Ted, the studio had decided to show film clips of a number of Paul's concert appearances. It was agony to watch him playing, to listen to his music filling her shabby room. Not only had his technique been masterful, but his depth of expression, the emotion he managed to evoke from the keyboard ranging from the most tender nuances to the vibrancy of deepest passion, brought tears to Christa's eyes. The glorious sounds he had created were stilled now, forever.

It was mentioned that since word of the accident and the resulting end of Paul Talbot's career had been released, sales of his records were soaring. There was a veritable stampede to obtain possession of them, and they were destined to become collectors' items.

Christa realized that she had several of them among the things Glenda had sent her from Boston, boxes which she had not yet unpacked because it had seemed, for a time, as if she might be shipping them right back to Massachusetts again.

She had no wish now, however, to go and get the records and play them on the venerable but still excellent record player that had at one time been her Uncle Julian's pride and joy, for to do so at the moment would be purely maudlin. Some day, perhaps, when the pain had lessened. . . .

The pain. There *was* indeed pain in connection with Paul, but this was not solely because of the crisis involving his music. The only conclusion that she had been able to come to lately was that he was studiously avoiding her during the hours she spent at the house working with his aunt, and this hurt. It very definitely hurt.

She wanted to ask Honora about him. She wanted to know if, for example, he simply was in the habit of getting up early and breakfasting by himself, and if that was why he never joined them for coffee. But Honora was too discerning. She would sense that more than curiosity about her nephew's eating habits was motivating Christa!

The Friday before Thanksgiving Honora developed a sore throat, and that morning she suggested Christa might spend the day working in the library, since she couldn't possibly "talk" her story.

Yesterday had been brilliantly sunny, and had this day been its counterpart Christa might have toyed with the idea of asking for the afternoon off, perhaps taking a long drive out into the country and stopping at an apple farm on the way back for some crisp macintoshes.

As it was, though, November had soured again. It was cold and very gray, charcoal clouds swelling ominously over the lake. Fitch had started a fire going in the library, and the flames cast golden shadows across the books, lovingly handled over the years, making their jewel-toned bindings glow. This was a wonderful room to work in, Christa told herself as she sat down behind the massive desk placed on an angle at the right side of the room, and started going over an accumulation of her notes. It would be a wonderful room to *share.* . . .

Even as she thought this, the door swung in, and Paul was almost to the center of the floor before he saw her.

He stopped short, and without even realizing what she was doing Christa stood up, the sheath of papers she had been handling slipping out of her fingers and scattering across the desk blotter.

He was wearing a heavy white turtleneck and snugly fitted dark blue slacks, and undoubtedly he had been making a regular thing of those walks along the lakefront because the hospital pallor was gone; his face, in fact, glowed with health, and he had never been more handsome.

Momentarily, he was as disconcerted as she was. Then he said politely, with a slight nod, "I'm sorry. I didn't know you were working in here or I wouldn't have disturbed you."

He turned and she knew that in another moment

he would be gone, and she couldn't let it happen like that.

She said, "Wait! Please. Why . . ."

That ironic eyebrow lifted. "Yes?" he suggested.

Christa moistened her lips. "Why," she managed to ask, the words coming painfully, "are you deliberately avoiding me?"

The other eyebrow rose to become level with the first one. "*Have* I been deliberately avoiding you?" he countered.

She felt as if her bones were slowly turning to jelly as his gray gaze swept over her coolly, even while he waited for her answer. For a moment, she nearly backtracked, but then she gritted her teeth, and forced herself to find the courage to speak.

"Must we play games with each other?" she asked him. "We are not children, after all. I don't think there's any doubt you've deliberately been avoiding me. Otherwise how could I spend the better part of eight hours a day in this house and never see you?"

"So you've noticed!" he said, with consummate sarcasm.

"How could I *help* but notice?" she flung back at him, his tone piquing her to anger. "I never see you, your aunt never speaks of you, neither do Martha or Fitch, for that matter, it's as if you weren't here at all!"

"Well," he asked her levelly, "isn't that the way you wanted it?"

"No!" she exploded, without even thinking. "You know perfectly well that isn't the way I wanted it. . . ."

The eyebrows, which had lowered, rose again, and his smile was purely taunting. "Oh, come on, now, Miss Emery," he said derisively. "Just what is this you're trying to tell me?"

He was looking at her in a way that was skeptical, at best, but what was even more galling was the definite twist of sardonic amusement to his lips, echoed by a gleam in his eyes as he came closer to the desk that seemed to hold more than a hint of laughter, for it was a kind of laughter, she knew, that would be purely derogatory as far as she was concerned.

She said stiffly, "I'm not trying to tell you *anything,* Mr. Talbot."

Now he did laugh, and the sound was every bit as derisive as Christa had expected it to be. He said, "I think you're one of those little girls who wants to have her cake and eat it too, and it doesn't work out that way. I didn't realize that a casual kiss could upset you so. . . ."

Again, her tongue betrayed her. "It wasn't a casual kiss!" she stormed, before she realized what she was saying.

"Wasn't it?" he taunted.

"To you, perhaps," she said testily, hating him for his attitude. "I suppose your life has been full of casual kisses. Mine hasn't been."

"The ultimate virgin, eh?" he commented. "Or perhaps I should say the eternal virgin? Is that what you're trying to tell me? Even so, I hardly assaulted your alleged honor. . . ."

She colored and, looking across at him, she was conscious, suddenly, of how she must appear to him. She hadn't bothered with makeup today, and she had twisted her blond hair into a workaday bun to keep it out of her face while she worked. Because of the dismal weather she had worn old clothes; a brown skirt that had seen better days, and a heavy, rose-colored velour pullover that had faded, but was still warm and comfortable.

While he had been getting out of doors she had been staying indoors, She knew that she was pale, and pallor did nothing at all to enhance her normally fair coloring. She had never felt plainer, nor had she ever been more tired. She had been tackling some hard physical jobs at the music school, and had been practicing the piano until well into the night, desperately needing the emotional release her music gave her. As a result, she was conscious of the fact that there were deep shadows under her eyes, and that she must appear decidedly wan and drawn, and this knowledge did nothing to enhance her morale.

He almost seemed to read her mind. He said abruptly, "You're losing weight."

This, too, was true. She seldom bothered with much in the way of dinner at night. She had discovered that it was no fun to cook for one person, and that eating alone could become a monotonous, in fact a downright dismal, experience.

He added, "You shouldn't lose weight. You've a nice figure, but you could do with a few added pounds."

The derision had faded, the gray eyes were steady and serious.

"It is really so difficult for you to come here and work, Christa?" he asked her. "Do you really dislike me that much?"

Dislike him! She did not dare look at him, for she was certain that if she did so, he would see in her eyes how completely wrong he was!

Knowledge swept through her like a warm tidal wave, devastating in its strength. She loved him! She loved him not as a hero-worshipping child but as a *woman!* This emotion that clutched her was no longer the adulation she had lavished either on the memory of a talented young man who had once taken her to the movies and bought her popcorn or, much more recently, on that striking figure who had so easily dominated an entire concert hall of clamoring wildly applauding people.

Everything she had known of Paul over the years, her early memories of him, all of this was background, yes; but, from that instant when they had confronted each other by the piano in the drawing room, there had been something entirely different, something that had culminated with that kiss which, on her part, could never be forgotten.

And on his part? She reminded herself that he was engaged to a beautiful and wealthy girl who surely would be arriving on the scene before much longer. And even if Gloria De Platte were not already in his life, there would be another woman like her; there must have been dozens of such women over the years, he had surely only to lift a finger and beckon. . . .

He was looking at her curiously. He said, "Can't you answer my question?"

She knew that she must sound as miserable and inadequate as she felt. She said, lamely, "I can't imagine why you would think I dislike you."

His smile was wry. "I can't imagine why I would think otherwise," he told her. "The very first time you met me you decided to resign your job here."

"That had nothing to do with you," she protested. "I mean—well, it did have to do with you, but . . ."

"I think I've mentioned before that you do have a way with words," he observed. "Just now you're stalling, however. Why don't you exercise your usual honesty and come out with what you have to say?"

Her legs were trembling so that she sat down behind the desk, again, and pressed them together as if this would serve to still them. Paul, with a slight shrug, sank into the armchair nearest the desk, and she was grateful for this. He seemed near Olympian when he stood while she sat; it was difficult enough to cope with him on a more even plane, she didn't need a semblance of some sort of ancient Grecian deity.

This, she knew, wasn't going to be easy. "Very well," she said. "The day Ted Bentley called and told your aunt about—about your accident, I began to realize that she undoubtedly would not want to continue with her book. . . ."

"Because of me?" The question came sharply.

"Well—yes."

"Did she feel that I would need that much coddling?" Paul asked bluntly.

"I don't know *what* she felt," Christa said desperately. "She was upset, of course, but she certainly didn't indicate . . ."

He interrupted her, his tone severe. "You're hedging again, Christa."

"I am *not* hedging, Paul!"

"I would advise you not to," he said ominously. "If I thought for a moment that my coming here imposed *that* kind of burden on Honora, I would go back to New York immediately!"

Christa stared at him, horrified. She had already managed in just a couple of sentences to give him the entirely wrong impression of the situation. He was assuming that she was speaking for Honora, and this was the farthest thing from the truth!

To her dismay, he got up and went to stand in front of the fireplace, his back to her. There was a tautness about him, he seemed to have become completely unapproachable, and this, she knew, was entirely her fault.

She forced herself to get up and walk around the end of the desk.

"Paul!" she said.

"Yes?" he answered, without turning.

"Believe me, you're coming to entirely the wrong conclusion, and it isn't fair to Honora. She dotes on you, you *must* know that! This is the only place in the world where she would want you to be right now. . . ."

"While I lick my wounds?" he demanded sarcastically.

The words thudded between them. Then Christa said, helplessly, "I can't answer you when you say things like that."

"I've noticed," he said, and now he swung around to face her, and his eyes were blazing. He said,

"You're *all* afraid to even mention the word music, and I get the feeling you all wish a magician would come in and wave a wand and make the piano in the drawing room disappear. It would be too *obvious* to have it moved out. . . ."

"Paul . . ."

"Look," he said, his voice tight, "let's face up to the truth, and that *is* the truth, isn't it? It has to be understood that no one can play a note on the piano while Paul is around, or even turn on a record. Honora acts like we don't even have a stereo in the family room, and as for you . . ."

"What *about* me?"

"When we were coming up from the lake that day I asked you if you were attending a conservatory and you nearly bit me."

"That," Christa said coldly, "had nothing to do with *you.*"

"Oh?" he inquired, with exaggerated politeness. "Do you really expect me to believe that you weren't trying to spare me the details of your musical prowess? Your Aunt Faith and I kept in touch over the years, you know, while I was at Juilliard and elsewhere and later when I started in on concert tours. She often wrote about you. There was no doubt in her mind that you were headed for the concert stage yourself. It's only three years since she died and you, if I'm correct about it, are approximately ten years younger than I am, which makes you not much over twenty-one. I would swear that Faith left money in her will for you to pursue your musical career. I suppose you're going to tell me I'm wrong about *that,* too."

"Extremely wrong," she said icily. "Aunt Faith put everything she had into the school. Her estate *was* the school, and it went to her husband. Oh, there was some cash, too, but that also went to Uncle Julian, and he was not about to finance my musical education with it. He had seen enough of poor musicians in the Emery family. He put me through secretarial school, and I was paying him back on a weekly basis when he died."

Paul was staring at her. "Why didn't you go to Honora?" he demanded. "Your aunt was like a sister to her. Honora would have seen that you went on with your studies. *I* would have seen that you went on with your studies, for that matter."

Their eyes locked, but for the moment there was no clash. "Christa," Paul began, but at the entirely wrong moment they were interrupted by a breezy new presence in the room.

"Whew!" said Ted Bentley, putting down a brief-case and tossing his topcoat over a corner chair. "That fireplace is an inviting sight! It's miserable out."

He walked toward the flames, warming his hands, "How's it going?" he asked, posing what was clearly a purely rhetorical question, for he didn't seem to notice that neither Christa nor Paul saw fit to answer him.

Chapter Seven

Christa had given little thought to the upcoming Thanksgiving holiday, and she was not prepared with a ready enough negative reply when Honora told her that she would, of course, be expected to come to the lakefront mansion for dinner.

She realized too late that if she had only thought about it in advance she could have asked for the holiday off and gone to Boston to spend the time with Glenda. As it was, any excuses she could offer for not joining Honora, Paul and Ted were feeble at best.

She and Paul had not been alone together since the afternoon in the library, and she could not help but ponder about how their dialogue might have developed if Ted had not arrived to interrupt it.

She had had no idea that her Aunt Faith had kept in such constant touch with her ex-pupil, even after he became a concert star, let alone that she had confided in him her hopes for Christa's future.

Paul clearly had been disconcerted by the revelation that she really was *not* studying music, and obviously had been extremely upset when he realized that this was because she had not been able to afford to do so.

She, for her part, had been astonished at his suggestion that she should have approached Honora

for help, and absolutely amazed when he had added
that he, himself, would have been equally willing to
come to her assistance.

He had, of course, been devoted to her Aunt Faith
in earlier years, she knew that; but she had assumed
that their relationship had diminished, once he left
Lakeport to return only for brief holidays.

She wished she could ask him if he and Faith ever
had met again, once he started to go on concert
tours, in fact she yearned to ask him many things
about the aunt she had loved so dearly. But, at
present, it seemed that whenever she did come upon
Paul at the house—and he was no longer making the
effort to stay out of her way that he had done prior to
that day in the library—Ted was with him.

Further, she often found Ted's eyes turned upon
her in a way that was somewhat upsetting. Other
young men, both in Albany and Boston, had at times
looked at her in that same way, and she recognized
the danger signals.

Ted Bentley was a pleasant young man, he was a
fun person to be around, but the last thing in the
world Christa wanted was for him to fancy that he
was in love with her.

As she was leaving the house one afternoon, just
prior to Thanksgiving, she met Paul and Ted coming
out of the library. She paused to chat with them for a
moment, then, when she said good-bye to Ted, he
lightly kissed her cheek. If it hadn't been for his
expression, she would have considered it more of a
brotherly gesture than anything else. Even as it was,
she didn't take it seriously, until she glanced at Paul.
Briefly, he looked as if a thundercloud had passed
across his face.

It was evident that Paul didn't favor a potential
romance between his manager and his aunt's
secretary—not that she had any intention of letting
such a situation develop. But, in a way, she resented
this. Did Paul think she was going to stay here and

work with Honora forever? Maybe he did at that, she decided ruefully, because it was becoming apparent that this project of Honora's could stretch on for a long, long while; as long as Honora wished, in fact.

The publisher had been more than liberal in allowing Honora a choice of a deadline, and even then had said that it would be "flexible," according to her wishes. Honora, for that matter, didn't seem to take the contract for her book all that seriously; she had even gone so far as to insist that no advance money be paid to her until the manuscript had been completed, evidently assuming that this gave her more latitude.

There were moments when Christa could not help but wish that the contract had been made a bit more binding. If she knew when the book had to be finished, then she could more easily begin to think of what she was going to do herself, when her position with Honora was over.

As it was, she was able to bank a large portion of her salary each week, and this meant that by spring she would be able to hire someone to paint the outside of the music school and do some of the interior work she couldn't handle herself.

Then—well, there would be time later to think about "then," she reminded herself, as she scanned the contents of her wardrobe the last Thursday of November, trying to decide what to wear in honor of Thanksgiving.

She wanted to look her best today, and finally she opted for a dress Glenda had persuaded her to purchase the previous winter, somewhat against her better judgment, because it was decidedly more expensive than her other dresses. It was a shade of antique gold that seemed to bring out hidden lights in her light blond hair, fashioned of soft, clinging material, with a fitted waistline that fully revealed the round curve of her breasts, and a scooped neckline that emphasized the lovely arch of her throat.

She took care with her makeup, adding a little eyeshadow, which she seldom wore, and she brushed her hair until it glistened like spun gold around her shoulders. She still had some of the delicious French perfume Glenda had given her last Christmas. Now she touched it to her earlobes and wrists, and felt herself enveloped in a glorious scent.

The final touch was an antique locket she had inherited from Aunt Faith, fashioned of heavy gold and centered with a gleaming topaz. She fastened this around her neck and had to admit, as she surveyed her own reflection in the old-fashioned, full-length mirror in the bedroom that, for once, she was pleased with what she saw!

Honora had told her not to drive over, insisting that someone would pick her up about three. She had expected that it would be Fitch who would come for her. To her surprise, however, when she answered the doorbell's ring it was Ted who stood on the threshold.

He put his hands over his eyes when he saw her, staggering backward with comic exaggeration.

"You're dazzling!" he told her, and she could not help but laugh at him.

As they drove out along the lake road in the sleek, silver Corvette, Ted asked, curiously, "What do you do with yourself evenings, alone in that big old barn?"

"Lots of things," she evaded.

"No time to spare?"

"There really isn't," she said, which, in a sense, was honest enough. "It doesn't seem as if I'll ever get finished. I've all sorts of projects."

"I can imagine," Ted said drily. "What I'm wondering is if you might have room for one more?"

She fell into the trap. "Such as?" she asked him.

"Me," he said succinctly.

She tried to make light of it. "Honestly, Ted," she protested, but he interrupted.

"I'm serious," he said. "At least, I'd *like* to be serious. I'm not an idiot, though. You're in love with Paul, aren't you."

He made it a statement, not a question, and she was completely shaken by it. She said, "I don't think you've the right to make an assumption like that."

"Perhaps I haven't," he conceded, "but if you continue in that vein I'm going to go into an old refrain and tell you that I think you protest too much, and that would be the truth, wouldn't it, Christa?"

"I've known Paul ever since I was twelve," she countered.

"And, all these years, you've cherished a sticky-sweet adolescent infatuation for him?" Ted suggested.

"No, I have *not!*" she said indignantly.

Ted said, placatingly, "There, now, I didn't mean to ruffle your feathers. They're entirely too pretty to be disturbed. I was probing, that's all. I'd like to know what *my* chances are. You can't blame me for that, can you?"

"You're *impossible!*" Christa said, forcing a light tone and an equally light laugh to go with it.

They were at the gates to the Talbot place now, and Ted turned into the driveway. He didn't speak until they were nearly at the front entrance, and then he said only one thing more, and he said it very seriously.

"Christa," his green eyes were serious, "I consider Paul my best friend, but in this short time you, too, have come to mean quite a lot to me. Take this as a warning, if nothing else. Don't let Paul burn you!"

Honora and Paul awaited them in the drawing room. Honora was wonderfully glamorous in floor-length bottle-green velvet, and Paul wore a superbly

tailored suit of a very dark gray, with a stark white
shirt and a discreetly patterned charcoal tie. Christa
had never seen him dressed so formally, except at
that concert appearance in Boston, and it was all she
could do to tear her eyes away from him.

The case on the grand piano had been closed, she
noted, the ivory keys were not visible. But there *was*
music, soft background music that, she realized, was
emanating from the stereo in the family room. She
suspected that Paul had come to the conclusion that
if no one else would play music around him, he
would put on a selection of records himself.

She noted, too, that there were tulip-shaped
champagne glasses set out on a coffee table. Honora
evidently had decided to make this Thanksgiving a
real occasion, and this was confirmed when Fitch
appeared bearing the champagne itself in a silver
bucket.

"Do you wish to do the honors, Mr. Paul?" Fitch
asked deferentially, and Paul nodded agreement,
taking the corkscrew opener and turning his attention toward the bottle.

Quite unconsciously, he drew it out of the bucket
with his left hand, preparing to hold it while he
unfastened the wire twisted about the stopper, then
to pop the cork itself with his right hand: and in an
instant disaster struck.

Paul's damaged hand clearly did not have the
strength to sustain a grip, and as they watched in
horror the bottle slid through his fingers and shat-
tered onto the rug.

Christa would never forget the moment that followed, nor the expression on Paul's face. Then she
reacted, rushing to him, taking his injured hand in
hers, and saying, as she looked down at it, "Oh, my
God! You didn't cut yourself, did you?"

She had never really *looked* at his hand before;
this had been something she had consciously
avoided. Now she saw that, just as Honora had

said, the scars were minimal. But the hand itself was limp, and virtually useless.

She glanced up to catch an expression of stark misery in his eyes that took him a moment to camouflage. Then he said very quietly, too quietly, "No, I didn't cut myself. Fitch, get another bottle, will you? And I think you or Ted had better handle the next one yourselves."

Martha came to sweep up the glass fragments, Honora said something bright and witty, and Ted switched into his best conversational form. In a very few minutes, only a damp area on the rug bore testimony to the mishap, yet Christa knew in her heart that something close to catastrophic had happened.

This was borne out when Paul drank more than his share of champagne and, as dinner was called, excused himself and went out to the kitchen. He rejoined the others quickly enough, but when he drew out her chair for her at the dining table Christa thought she could smell the strong odor of whiskey on his breath.

Two different kinds of wine were served with Martha's excellent dinner, which included turkey with a special kind of sausage and pecan stuffing, both whipped potatoes and candied sweet potatoes, scalloped oysters, creamed broccoli, crisp celery and deliciously crunchy toasted almonds, the inevitable cranberry sauce, and a choice of pumpkin or mince pie for dessert.

This was followed by coffee and brandy, and Christa noticed that whereas Paul had refused seconds on the food he was now helping himself liberally to the brandy.

When they returned to the drawing room, he requested Fitch to bring in another decanter of brandy, and for the first time Honora looked faintly apprehensive.

Ted, attempting a diversion, said, "Why don't we

all go out for a walk and work off some of that dinner?"

Paul's smile was ironic. "In case you haven't noticed," he pointed out, "it's been sleeting for the past two hours."

He finished the contents of the glass he was holding, and refilled it. Then, to her consternation, he nodded toward the grand piano and said to Christa, "How about playing something?"

She flinched visibly. "Thank you, no," she said.

"Why not?" Paul persisted.

"I'd rather not."

"Why would you rather not?" he kept on, and there was an ugly note in his voice.

"Paul," Honora protested, but he ignored his aunt.

"Possibly," he said, "we could do a duet with 'Chopsticks.' I *can* use my right hand, you know."

"Please," Christa said, the word little more than a whisper.

His eyes raked her. "Have you no guts?" he asked her scathingly. He went to the piano, flung back the lid, his hand hitting the keys as he did so, the discordant notes that resulted seeming to smite the very air itself. The stereo long since had ceased playing. In the wake of the piano notes dying out there was an intense stillness in the room, an absolutely *audible* stillness.

Paul turned to her, repeating the question tauntingly. "I asked you," he said, "if you simply have no guts? What is wrong with you? What do you think I'm going to do if you sit down and play this thing? Chop your hands off?"

It was Ted who stood up now, starting forward. "Paul," he said, his own voice low, and just barely under control. "You're going too far, don't you think?"

"With *her?*" Paul asked, scorchingly, staring at

Christa and then seeming to dismiss her in a single glance. "Not as far as you've probably gone!"

"I'd like to know what you mean by that!" Ted said, dangerously quiet now.

It was Honora who spoke, sharply. "Paul," she exclaimed. "Ted! What is the matter with both of you? What must Christa think? This isn't the first time you've owed her an apology, Paul, and I think you'd better make one immediately."

Paul's smile was highly unpleasant. "No," he agreed, "it isn't the first time, is it? And I don't imagine it will be the last. But I'm not about to apologize for anything until I know why she refuses to play for me."

Christa felt herself awash in misery. She raised haunted eyes to him, and for a brief moment she thought she was reaching him. She said, "I don't want to play for you because I'm not in practice."

He shook his head in disgust. As she watched, he refilled his brandy glass with his good right hand, then all but waved it in Christa's face.

"You," he told her, "are a liar!" And, as they all three stared at him in horror, he left the room carrying his brandy, and a moment later they heard his footsteps receding up the stairs.

Thanksgiving had turned into a fiasco, and in the days that followed Paul managed to make himself invisible while Christa was in the Talbot house. She wondered if she could continue to stand the tension of being in the same place with him without knowing where he was, what he was doing, what he was thinking.

Why had he accused her of lying about her playing? Why had he even *wanted* to hear her play, for that matter? It simply didn't make sense. Then, there was the matter of his comment to the effect that Ted had undoubtedly "gotten further" with her than he had, and her cheeks burned with resentment at the memory of this.

Honora was right! He did owe her another apology, but he certainly didn't seem about to proffer it.

The stores in town had been decorated for Christmas, beaming Santa Clauses in bright red suits jangled their bells on street corners, the festive season had arrived.

The tinsel garlands and colored lights strung out across the streets from store building to store building admittedly looked tawdry in the daytime, but with darkness they seemed to become enchanted with a shining, promising beauty that made anyone with any feeling at all want to be a part of this lovely time of the year.

Christa, however, felt more devoid of Christmas spirit than she had ever been before; thus, when one evening she was sitting at her piano playing Beethoven's sonata *Pathétique*, she put into the music all her suppressed emotions. Her personal sorrow spilled over, giving her playing a power and vibrancy of which she was quite unaware.

She was midway through the rondo when she heard a distinct rustling outside the studio window, and, although she was not easily alarmed, this, she knew immediately, was not a sound being made by the wind or by an animal, but by a human!

The thought that there was someone standing outside her window was a chilling one. She forced herself to continue with her playing, even though her fingers fumbled on some of the notes as she did so. She executed a trill, fingered a chord, then paused, hoping that she was giving her eavesdropper the impression that she was studying the beginning of the tranquillo section. Then very quietly she slipped away from the piano, tiptoeing through the studio and across the vestibule.

She opened the old double doors carefully, hoping they wouldn't creak. Outside it had begun to snow, the flakes falling gently but steadily. Christa had always loved the first snow of the season; now she caught her breath at the sight of it. Then she concentrated on her mission, peering cautiously around the corner of the door.

Although she had drawn the curtains in the studio, as she always did at night, they were not totally opaque. The light from the lamp by her piano filtered through them, spilling ivory radiance out into the frosty night.

In its glow, she saw the silhouette of a man, pressed close to the studio window!

Common sense warned her that she should go to the phone immediately and call the police, yet she found herself edging forward. There was something very familiar about that silhouette—and as she advanced a little further she confirmed her own identification. It was Paul!

Even as she decided this he turned and saw her, and immediately started toward her. Christa's option for retreat was instinctive, but she had forgotten about the holly bushes that edged the sides of the front step. She stumbled as she felt a leaf prick at her ankle, and would have fallen if Paul had not moved, swiftly, to catch her in his arms.

He held her for a long moment, staring down at her in the dimness as the snow anointed her upturned face and sprinkled frosty touches on his dark hair. Then, when she thought she couldn't bear it any longer, his mouth closed upon hers in a kiss that was as infinitely tender and gentle as the first kiss he had ever given her had been savage.

Christa lost all sense of time as he held her and kissed her, the snow thickening meanwhile until both of them were wearing more than a slight mantle of it. She knew only that she wished there never again *needed* to be a sense of time, that she could simply remain here within the circle of his arms forever.

Then slowly, reluctantly, he released her. His glance encompassed the blouse and skirt she was wearing, with only a light sweater added for warmth.

"Good God," he said, "You'll get pneumonia!"

Before she could speak, he drew her toward the open doorway, pushing her ahead of him into the vestibule.

"Are you soaked through?" he demanded.

"Not really," she said, brushing away the snow. "Are you?"

"Just my parka," he admitted, removing it and spreading it out over a stiff-backed wooden chair. "And my hair has been dryer, but then so has yours."

She found herself saying, "I've a fire going in the studio. We can dry out there in no time. I can't offer you any brandy but I can make some cocoa for us, if you'd like."

His lips twisted wryly. "That sounds rather as if you've come to the conclusion that I'm addicted to brandy—or alcohol, shall we say?"

Must he always needle her? "I didn't mean *that*. . . ." she began, but he laughed, a perfectly natural and pleasant laugh.

"Don't let me provoke you so easily!" he told her. "As a matter of fact, I'd love a cup of cocoa, and I would say that considering my behavior the last time we spoke to each other you're pretty decent to offer it to me."

She could feel that telltale flush mounting again, and she wished fervently that she could control the effect he had on her. She said, "You had a right to be upset Thanksgiving Day."

"Because I was clumsy?" He said, "Christa, we can't simply *forget* this hand of mine, there's no point in pretending it doesn't exist and isn't of much use to me. I handled the situation badly at Thanksgiving, and I'm willing to admit I deserved a swift kick instead of sympathy. However, once I'd had too much to drink what infuriated me especially was that you refused to play for me. I still can't understand why you lied about being in practice."

"Because I'm not!"

He put his finger on her chin, and tilted it upward. He looked down into her very deep blue eyes and said, "You really *believe* that, don't you?"

"Yes."

"Then I do owe you an apology. I don't happen to agree, but that's beside the point. The reason I thought you were lying to me, you see, is that I've listened to you play on a number of evenings, standing outside your studio window. . . ."

"What?"

His smile was wistful. He said, "Ever since I came home, you've been my only music, Christa."

There was a poignancy to both the smile and the words that Christa found especially tearing.

"I suppose," he continued, "this makes me seem like some sort of a Peeping Tom. But I knew if I came to the door you'd refuse to go on playing, and that's so, isn't it?"

She said very slowly, "Yes—I suppose it is."

"I wish you would tell me—*honestly*—the real reason."

"I *have*," she said, and was distressed to see his eyebrows raise, in that ironic way, and an expression of pure cynicism come to linger around his mouth.

"Look," she said quickly, "maybe you're not cold but I am! Come out to the kitchen while I make the cocoa, and then we can go and sit in front of the fire in the studio and I'll try to explain why I—why I couldn't possibly be comfortable playing in front of you."

She was more than slightly surprised at herself after she made this speech. She was, she realized, treating Paul Talbot as if he were someone her own age, someone who lived within her own orbit. But it was a treatment that seemed to work.

He followed her into the old-fashioned kitchen, pulling out a wooden chair and sitting down at the much used round table.

Watching her making the cocoa he said reflectively, "This brings back a great many memories."

"I should imagine it might."

"I don't mean just the school itself, Christa," he said, "though that's certainly brim full of memories for me. If it hadn't been for your Aunt Faith, I never would have had the guts to apply to Juilliard. I mean this kitchen. Your Aunt Faith used to bring me out here after lessons—that was before you ever moved here—and she'd make cocoa for me, and she always had a plate of home-baked cookies."

"I'm afraid I can't follow through in that respect."

"Where were you then, Christa?"

"How long ago would this have been?"

"I started taking lessons from her before you were born," he said simply. "I started when I was about nine, to be precise. But I'm talking, now, about the time when I was, say somewhere between twelve and maybe sixteen. You would have been a toddler. . . ."

"I was in kindergarten by the time you were sixteen!" she said defiantly.

He laughed at this. He said, "Okay. So you were practically grown up! Did you live here in Lakeport?"

"Part of the time," Christa said. "My father was a violinist—but he never really made it, even though he had a great deal of talent."

"Many people with a great deal of talent *don't* ever make it."

"Sometimes my father had a chance to play with orchestras in various places—minor cities, I guess you'd say. He never appeared in New York or London or any of the places you've been. . . . The summer I was twelve we were back here," she continued.

"That must have been while I was still at Juilliard," he mused. "I went to Majorca that summer with an English friend whose family had a place at Formentor."

"Yes, you were at Juilliard," she agreed. "Aunt Faith talked a great deal about you. You were the most brilliant student she ever had."

He didn't answer this, and she turned, hoping that she had not, now, said entirely the wrong thing to him, only to find him regarding her speculatively.

"I'm not so sure about *that*," he said, "but we'll let it pass for the moment. Go on about the summer when you were twelve."

She turned off the stove, and removed the pot of steaming cocoa. She said, carefully, "My parents were out in a boat—and a sudden squall came up. My mother couldn't swim at all. My father tried to rescue her. They were both drowned."

She heard him push back the chair. He said, his voice husky, "My God, Christa, I'm sorry. I should have realized! What a clod I was to put the question to you that way!"

She was pouring the cocoa, her hand steadier than her voice. She said, "Please! You couldn't be expected to remember. I've long since grown—used to it. I can talk about it now, believe me. . . ."

"I believe you," he said, "but there's one thing you might elaborate on. Why shouldn't I be expected to remember?"

She shrugged impatiently. She said, "You went on to other things, a whole different world."

"To become bathed in glory, is that it?" he asked, an odd note in his voice.

"Please!" she said, again. "Let's take the cocoa into the studio, shall we?"

She had poured the cocoa into two fragile Limoges cups. She said, "There's enough for a second cup for both of us, but I'll come back and reheat it."

He walked around the table, and once again he

put his finger under her chin and tilted her face upward. As she wondered what he was about to do next, he bent and kissed her lips very lightly.

He said gently, "You're hedging again, Christa. But someday, perhaps, you'll be bathed in glory yourself, and then you'll realize there is a great deal that is phony behind those footlights. I'm not speaking about the music. The music is something else. But it was your Aunt Faith who instilled in me the essential truth that adulation and applause are not always measured out in equal proportion to that quality we call talent."

He smiled down at her rather sadly. "I don't think you even know what I'm talking about!"

"Perhaps I do," she told him. She handed him his cocoa and preceded him into the studio, settling herself in one chair by the fire and waiting for him to take the other one. But, to her amazement, he put down his cup, went over to the old piano and, with his right hand, ran a *glissando* that made her want to cry out loud, because the very sweep of it showed that he still had that *something*. . . .

He said, "She taught me my first scales on this," then picked up his cocoa, and came to sit in the chair across from her.

Christa could feel a thickening lump in her throat, but she said only, very slowly, "She taught me my first scales on it, too."

"I think," Paul said, sipping the cocoa, "that she would be pleased at the thought we're here in this room together."

"Yes," Christa agreed, then plunged on without even thinking, "Except that she would be terribly upset about . . ."

She let the rest of the sentence drop off, and she was afraid to even look at him. But he finished, quietly, "About me?"

"Yes."

A long moment of silence fell between them.

Then he said, "If she *were* here, what do you think she'd suggest?"

An odd feeling came over Christa. She knew that this was no idle question and that her own answer to it was tremendously important, so important, in fact, that the sense of responsibility even the *thought* of forming an answer gave her was overwhelming.

But she had known her Aunt Faith. So she said, steadily, "I think she would tell you that you must— go on. And that you must *do* something with your life."

He stared at her, and she could not begin to read his expression. But he said, "I think you're right. And I may, Christa, I just may, follow the advice your Aunt Faith would have given me."

Chapter Eight

Christa did not see Paul at the house the next day. But the following morning, she found him sitting in the breakfast room with Honora when she arrived, having coffee and some of Martha's freshly baked apple muffins.

Honora said, with an upraised eyebrow that reminded Christa forcibly of Paul, "My nephew has made a request, but I think it's up to you to make a decision about it."

Paul frowned. "I wouldn't exactly call that cooperation, Honora," he said coolly.

His aunt frowned back at him. "I'm not exactly sure I want to cooperate," she said. "The whole thing is entirely up to Christa."

Christa stared from Honora to Paul and back to Honora again, entirely mystified and gaining no clues from either of them. Then Honora, taking pity on her, said, "He wants me to work on my own notes this morning while you play for him."

She was staggered. *"Why?"* she demanded.

Paul said, tantalizingly, "I'll tell you why after you do it. Damn it, Honora, you could have been a little bit more . . ."

"Helpful? I'm not sure about that," Honora told him loftily. "Sometimes it isn't the wisest thing to dabble in someone else's life. . . ."

"Damn it!" Paul exploded. "Do you really think I'm about to *dabble?*"

Honora shrugged. "I haven't had an opportunity to analyze your motivation," she said, being even more tantalizing than Paul had been. "However, you are a Talbot, you might remember that *I* am a Talbot, and I think I understand the way the family mind sometimes runs."

Paul glared at her. "You might explain what you mean by *that!*"

Honora merely shrugged again, a bit more elaborately this time.

"I shall give you your chance," she said enigmatically. "The morning is all yours. I'll see you at lunchtime, Christa." And, before Christa could recover, she arose and stalked, majestically, from the room.

Now that they were alone, it was Christa's turn to face Paul across the table, and her prime feeling at the moment was one of intense annoyance. She had no wish to become a pawn between Honora and Paul, even though she had absolutely no idea of what this particular chess game involved!

Evidently Paul had a downright *obsession* to have her play for him, and this she simply could not understand.

He was looking at her impatiently, and he said, "Aren't you *ever* going to finish that coffee?"

This was the last comment she had expected and she stared at him blankly and asked, "Why?"

"Well," he said reasonably, "Honora *has* given us the morning, but I think she's made it pretty clear she wants you for herself this afternoon. Drink up, and let's go into the drawing room, shall we?"

Christa shook her head, exasperated. "Why," she demanded, "are you being so *persistent* about this? It doesn't make sense!"

"It does to me," he told her.

He stood, "Come *on*," he said, and she had the feeling that she was standing next to a tiger, tensed and ready to spring. "Your coffee's cold, anyway."

He strode toward the drawing room. Christa stared at his retreating back helplessly, then slowly, reluctantly, followed him.

He had already thrust back the cover from the keys of the piano, and was propping up the top. He wanted full sound and effect, she realized dismally, and she felt woefully unprepared to give him either.

He drew out the bench for her with an elaborate gesture. "Well?" he asked, that ironic eyebrow arching up again.

She looked down at this beautiful instrument which she had remembered so fondly for so many years and, briefly, she hated it. Her anger rose against Paul for his cavalier treatment, and, childishly, she wanted to kick the bench he was holding for her.

He was waiting for something he had absolutely no right to wait for. Music was an extremely *personal* thing, at least to her, and he above all people should respect that, she thought angrily. True, if one was a professional then the instrument in question must be played regardless of moods or circumstances. But she was *not* a professional, and Paul knew it!

He asked, almost lazily, "Why the sparks?"

"Because, damn it," she said, "I am *not* going to play for you!"

"The hell you're not!" he told her, and before she knew what was happening he was literally thrusting her down onto the piano bench, then pushing the bench into place.

He pulled up a nearby chair, and she knew very well that she had no escape route. She glared at him. She said, "I've never known of anyone being *forced* to play an instrument!"

"I've never known anyone to be so stubborn about agreeing to a simple request," he countered.

"It's not a simple request . . ." she began impetuously.

"No?"

"Of course it's not! Are you so totally dense that you can't imagine how I would feel playing for *you?*"

The second eyebrow rose. He said, "May I ask if you mean that as a *personal* 'you' or a *professional* 'you'?"

"Oh, what do you think?" she asked him angrily.

He gave her a glance of pure irritation. "It really wouldn't do much good to tell you what *I* think," he said, "if you are going to persist in acting like a star struck little idiot!"

At that she pushed back the bench, nearly knocking it into his legs, and sprang to her feet.

"I am *not* a star struck little idiot," she stormed at him. "Right now I don't have much respect for the '*personal* you,' since you put it that way, but I *do* respect the '*professional* you.' I was at your concert in Boston last year, but even if I hadn't been, I know just as anyone else who knows anything at all about music knows that you're probably the greatest concert pianist to have come along in years. . . ."

The expression on his face stopped her, and only now, looking down at him, did she fully realize what a mask he had been wearing ever since he came back to Lakeport.

Honora had suspected that her nephew was putting up a very good front, and she was only too correct! Right now the pain in Paul's eyes was so intense that Christa wanted desperately to throw her arms around him and try to comfort him. But this, she knew instinctively, would never do; not with Paul. He would translate it as pity, and pity was something he would despise.

How could she cope? How could she help him? The questions converged one upon the other, and she closed her eyes tightly, wrestling with her own emotions, only to open them when he said quietly,

"Put it in the past tense, Christa. It's over, and you're right. It was presumptuous of me to try to bully you into playing for me. I chose this admittedly forceful approach because obviously you have quite a hangup about it. I don't know whether you feel that because I've been a professional I'll be super critical of anything you do—or just what your reasons are. But, regardless, you have a right to them."

He hesitated. "At your house the other night," he reminded her, "you said that if your Aunt Faith could give me advice, she would urge me to do something with my life. You should know that *that's* what I've had in mind in being so insistent about wanting you to play."

She frowned. "I don't understand you."

"I told you I've *heard* you playing—standing there outside your studio window. True, although I've been a student and a performer myself, I've never been a teacher. But I think you have far more talent than you realize, and I also think I could help bring it out. Honora has agreed to let us have the mornings, working on your music, and then you can work with her in the afternoons."

"What *point* would there be to it?" Christa asked desperately.

"To prepare you for the concert stage," he told her.

The afternoon after she finally played for Paul, Christa approached Honora's boudoir with mixed feelings, for it seemed to her that what was happening was not quite fair to her employer.

Honora, after all, had hired her to help get out a book. Now, if her time were to be cut in half, she must make sure that Honora felt she could cope with this, and also there must be an adjustment made in salary. This, admittedly, was worrisome.

She had counted on working with Honora through

the winter and probably into spring, realizing that, the way they were going, it would certainly take that long to finish the autobiography.

This would mean that *by* spring she should be able to save enough so that the house could be painted and at least some of the other necessary repairs effected.

If she were to work for Honora *half* time, though, she should certainly be paid only half the amount she was now receiving. For that matter, she had felt from the very beginning that Honora was overpaying her, in any event.

There was no chance that first afternoon to discuss finances with Honora because the older woman had amassed material she wanted to "talk out," and she kept Christa busy with her informal type of dictation until after five o'clock.

The following morning, however, Christa went to the house with the firm intention of talking things out with Honora over coffee in the breakfast room, before she started on any sort of lesson program with Paul.

To her dismay, she found that Paul was alone at the table, and when she asked about Honora, he replied casually that she had opted to have a tray in her room this morning.

Christa was certain that this gesture had been a deliberate one. Honora, she knew, would do anything for Paul. Still, she *did* have prior rights to her own secretary-assistant!

Paul poured coffee for her, and as she sipped it she said, "I must tell you, in all honesty, that I still feel very uncertain about this teaching project of yours."

He actually grinned at her. "No faith in me as a maestro?" he asked.

"It isn't that at all! I do have a prior allegiance to Honora, though, and I haven't had the chance to discuss this with her at all."

"Because I've been so high-handed?"

"Well, you haven't been *exactly* meek," Christa told him flatly. "I don't think you've *asked* anyone anything. You simply made up your own mind about what was going to be done and expected everyone else to fall in with you."

"Progress," Paul observed with satisfaction.

"What do you mean by *that?*"

"I mean that a while ago you would never have taken me to task. I like to think it's an indication you may be getting the courage to say what you think."

"It wouldn't occur to me that you'd doubt my courage in *that* department," Christa snapped back. "Other times, you've accused me of saying too much. . . ."

"Yes," he conceded, "but your most vocal expressions have been when you were angry. This morning, though, you're not angry—or are you?"

He asked this teasingly, and it had the effect of again making her feel as if her cheeks were turning scarlet.

"No," she said, almost shortly. "I'm not angry."

"But you will be if I keep this up?" Paul was making no secret of the fact that he was enjoying this interchange. "Okay. Go on up and talk to Honora. Matter of fact, I think I'll come with you."

"Thank you, but no," Christa said firmly. "I'd prefer to talk to her by myself."

"My, but you do trust me!" he mocked. "Talk away, then, but please do take a message to her from me."

"What message?" she asked suspiciously.

"I think a different schedule might work out better," he said, "depending upon how much your work with Honora tires you."

She frowned. "What is that supposed to mean?"

"Exactly what I said. *Does* your work with Honora tire you?"

"No. As a matter of fact, I find it stimulating. It's a great deal of fun to work for her, everything she's done, everything she is putting in the book, is so exciting and exotic it's like plunging into a whole pool of vicarious glamour."

"Do you need vicarious glamour in your life, little one?"

Now she did flush. She said, "You seem to have an endless capacity for latching onto one single phrase and . . ."

"And what?"

"And making too much of it," Christa said definitely.

He was wearing the Irish sweater that he had been wearing when he kissed her down by the lakefront. She glanced unthinkingly at the neckline, for she was certain that she had gotten lipstick on it, and he chuckled.

"It came out," he said succinctly. "Okay, okay. Don't bite me, please. Or hit me. You might bruise your hand, and we need those fingers."

She nearly gasped when he said this, thinking of his own hand, but he regarded her imperturbably. "You haven't asked me what my new plan is," he pointed out, "and I *would* like to have you check it out with Honora."

"Well, what is it?" she asked, deliberately brusque.

"I think that it would be best if you work with Honora mornings. After lunch—on good days at least—we'll take a walk so that you can store up a little oxygen, and on bad days rest for an hour or so. Then we can shut ourselves up in the drawing room with the piano until it's time for a pre-dinner drink. After you've had dinner, I'll drive you home—I'm not too keen about your driving yourself, this time of the year, it's apt to be icy after dark. That means, obviously, that either Fitch or I will pick you up in the morning, which I think would be a good idea anyway because that car you inherited from your uncle is on its last wheels."

Would he never cease to surprise her? "Oh," she said, with feigned politeness, "so you've investigated my car, too?"

"Yes. Having had a rather miserable experience in a car myself, I'm a bit touchy about transportation," he told her firmly. "In the event you're afraid I'll try to come into your house and make a nuisance of myself when I take you home evenings, I can assure you that I won't even darken your door. That's why I intend to see you home myself, especially after Bentley gets back from his latest trek to New York. I wouldn't trust him to let you go so easily."

"I see."

"I'm not sure you do, but it's the way it will have to be. You're not going to have time for romantic flings, shall we say, or anything else that falls into the general social area."

"Romantic flings fall into a *social* area?"

"That's a matter of opinion," Paul said carelessly. "To continue with my outline of our proposed program so that you can present it to Honora, after I take you home I expect you to practice for precisely two hours before you go to bed."

"Are you going to have the house equipped with some sort of video device so you can be sure I'm not disobeying you?" she demanded impertinently.

"That might not be a bad idea."

She finished her coffee, and gazed at him levelly.

"What if I don't go along with this?" she suggested. "What if I feel that even if Honora does favor this new program of yours it would be better to have the lessons in the morning, as we planned originally?"

"Then I would have to convince Honora that I've thought it out and mine is the better way."

"You're so sure of that?" she taunted. "This *is* her house, you know, and there's absolutely no reason why I should be served dinner here every evening."

"On the contrary," he said with suspicious politeness, "there is. You've said your work with Honora doesn't tire you. Your work with me will. You'll be ready for some sherry before dinner, and a good hot dinner, and even at that it's going to be hellishly hard for you to put in those two extra hours on the piano before you go to bed, as you'll find out.

"Even if that weren't so, though, I'd insist you stay to dinner anyway. I don't want you coming down with the first virus that drifts your way simply because you're undernourished."

"I am *not* undernourished!" Christa told him indignantly.

"I think you are. Now run along and talk to Honora, will you, and unless she's planned something else for her morning we might as well get the right schedule started today.

"In which event," he concluded, reaching for the copy of the local morning paper which Fitch had brought in, "I'll be seeing you at lunch."

Honora, somewhat to Christa's dismay, was pleased rather than upset by Paul's proposed change in schedule, and thoroughly delighted with the entire concept of the lesson program.

Honora, in fact, was the "old" Honora once again; she seemed more totally herself than she had since that terrible morning when Ted Bentley had phoned with the word of the accident.

This attitude on the older woman's part, however, only strengthened Christa's misgivings.

"Frankly, Honora, I simply can't see this," she said. "I think it has become a fixation with Paul."

"You think he's using you as a vehicle to assuage his own frustrations?" Honora suggested.

"Yes, that's exactly what I do think. I'll never be a concert artist, and I know it. He's being stubborn and illogical about the whole thing."

"He's also coming back to life," Honora said simply. "We've had a few very deep talks, Paul and I, when we've been here alone, nights," she confessed. "He has gone through hell, he's still going through hell, but you've already helped him more than you'll ever know."

Christa frowned. She said, "I don't mean to seem cruel—and I would do—well, I would do a great deal for Paul. I sympathize with him more than I can say. But I don't relish being used as a kind of therapy. This is a fantasy sort of thing. It's bound to come to an end, and it seems to me that if you believe in a fantasy and then you find out you've merely been following some kind of pink balloon and it bursts, the letdown would be tremendous. He would truly crash. Do you think it's wise to get into something like that?"

Honora had been watching her very closely, and Christa realized, uncomfortably, that Honora's hazel eyes could be every bit as sharp as Paul's gray ones could be.

She said, "Why are you so sure that this is fantasy, Christa? I think you underestimate both yourself and Paul's potential as a teacher. Also, although I probably shouldn't say this to you, it seems to me that your attitude is rather selfish. Is it asking so much for you to bring music into his life again even if, as you suggest, it does prove to be a pink balloon in the end, and the balloon bursts? If that happens, Paul will have had the adjustment time he badly needs, and I think he will also have found a direction in which to gear his own life."

Honora also had the capacity to get things her own way, Christa realized, just as Paul did. Nevertheless, she said, "I don't think that my reluctance to do this stems from selfishness, and I'll stand by that. I just think it's the wrong kind of an involvement. You're as much as saying that I'm being used as a form of therapy. Do you think that's fair?"

"Fair to whom?" Honora posed lightly. "To Paul or yourself?"

It would have been enough to stand up against either Paul or Honora, but when the two of them were in accord, the effort required was bound to be almost too enormous, Christa decided.

Thus, she spent the morning working with Honora, and it proved to be a particularly enjoyable session because today Honora detailed some of the experiences she had had while singing at La Scala in Milan, and they were hilarious.

They were both still laughing as they came downstairs to lunch, to find Paul waiting for them in the foyer. As he looked up and directly into her eyes he smiled, and Christa nearly missed a step. She caught herself up quickly, but this was, she decided, a kind of warning. She must *watch* her step with Paul, or, regardless of the outcome of his proposed study program, her heart was going to suffer damage that she knew very well she could never possibly recover from.

As they walked toward the dining room, Paul said, "You look as if a cloud suddenly came across your face just now. Why?"

He was entirely too perceptive. She said, "It was nothing, really."

"You never reveal your thoughts, do you, Christa?"

"I wouldn't say that."

Honora had gone ahead of them. They reached the table, and since Honora was already seating herself Paul pulled out Christa's chair for her. She brushed him as she sat down, and at this mere touch a tingling sensation swept over her. She knew that, briefly, her face mirrored her emotions, and she quickly glanced toward Honora and was dismayed to find that her employer had, indeed, been watching them.

Did Honora suspect that she was in love with Paul? Christa wondered.

Martha had prepared a delicious chicken casserole, laced with slivered toasted almonds and garnished with whole green grapes. Christa and Honora had been accustomed to having either a sandwich or a salad during their luncheons together, and Christa could not help but wonder if this more substantial fare was Paul's idea. He did, indeed, seem determined to fatten her up!

Lunch over, he glanced out the window and said briefly, "Exercise time. Is your coat in the closet?"

"Yes," she said, "but I can get it."

"So can I," he informed her. "Honora, it wouldn't do you any harm to take a brisk walk along the lake."

"Thank you just the same," Honora said, "but I'm old enough to indulge myself and you know perfectly well that I'm incredibly lazy. I plan to spend my afternoon reading, and enjoying a brief siesta. I'll meet you both for sherry before dinner."

As they left the house and started down the gravel path Paul glanced at Christa's feet and said approvingly, "I see you've worn flats. That's a good idea. No stumbling on the stones today, okay?"

Was this a way of conveying the message that there was not to be a repeat of their original lakefront walk? That, in short, he did not expect her to cause an incident which, in turn, would demand that he catch her in his arms, leading to yet another, bruising kiss?

Thinking about this, Christa marched along stiffly.

Had he *possibly* thought that she had stumbled *deliberately* that first time?

The mere idea made her fume, and she watched her footing with special care. He need not fear, she told herself, that there was going to be a repeat performance!

Chapter Nine

Paul had been right in his choice of a time slot for their lessons. Each afternoon, by the time he had finished with her, Christa was more than ready to join Honora in the family room, where Fitch would already have placed the decanter of sherry and the thin-stemmed wine glasses on the coffee table.

Invariably, there would be a fire blazing on the hearth, and there was a growing warmth and intimacy among the three of them, Christa realized, that would surely cause trauma for *her*, at least, when, one day the pink balloon finally burst, as she was sure it eventually must.

Paul had also been right about her need to eat a good dinner, in view of the schedule he was keeping her to. The delicious, nourishing food Martha provided was making her begin to put on weight, but this was something she surely did not have to worry about. She was looking better than she had in a long time, despite her stern, demanding taskmaster—or, perhaps, because of him!

Except on those days when the weather was really bad, they took their walk after lunch, and came back to begin the afternoon's lessons with their cheeks ruddy and their eyes sparkling. On those walks, though, they said very little to each other, and Christa continued to wear either flats or boots, as the weather demanded, and to make extremely sure that she didn't stumble!

The physical exercise she soon realized, was a mere preliminary to the completely different type of exertion that followed when he stood over her at the piano, making her repeat chord after chord, phrase after phrase, even note after note.

Occasionally he would finger a passage that she was not getting, using his right hand; but his mastery was painfully evident in even this limited amount of playing.

Sometimes she would go upstairs for a final word with Honora when they returned from their after lunch walk and one afternoon, when she returned to the drawing room, she found Paul seated at the piano, running his right hand idly over the keys, picking out a melody that had about it a particularly haunting theme.

When she asked him what it was, he said casually, "Oh, nothing in particular." He played a final *arpeggio,* and then he said, "Too bad, in a way, that it wasn't my right hand, even though I *am* extremely right-handed. There have been some pretty good things written for piano for just the left hand alone, though. . . ."

Although he spoke matter-of-factly, a poignancy came through this statement that brought a lump to her throat and, to her horror, her eyes filled with tears. He turned and saw them, and his mouth twisted.

"No, Christa," he said thickly. "Not your pity! Not that."

She bit her lip, but she couldn't stem the tears, and she turned away from him, trying, fiercely, to fight down her emotions. In a moment he was behind her, swinging her back toward him, and he said, harshly, "I mean that. I don't want pity! Not yours, not anyone's! Can't you understand that?"

She said, choking out the words, "It isn't *pity*. . . ."

"The hell it isn't!" he contradicted her roughly.

But she only shook her head. "Paul, *please*," she said. "You can't always hide the way you feel. Sometimes, you've got to let it out. . . ."

His arms tightened about her, his gray eyes darkened, and this time, when his lips found hers, there was passion and tenderness melded together in his kiss, in a fusion that made her tremble from head to foot. She found herself pressing her body against his, knowing a mounting elation from the very *feel* of him. She realized that with him she was powerless; were he to sweep her up in his arms and take her *anywhere*, at this moment, it would be impossible to resist him!

But even as her own senses were soaring and her responses deepening, he thrust her away from him, almost angrily.

"*That*," he said, "I definitely don't want. Give your charity to someone else, Christa! There's no place for this sort of thing between us."

She noted the jaw muscle twitching in his cheek, and saw that his mouth had become so taut there was a thin white line around his lips. She couldn't imagine how *she* looked; she knew only that he had all but devastated her with that single, harsh phrase.

"*Give your charity to someone else.*"

How could he *possibly* think that her response to him could fall into the category of *charity*? How could he think that she would yield to *anyone* else as she had just now yielded to him?

She felt cold all over and when, to her astonishment, he said, as if nothing had happened between them, "Let's get to work," she turned to him, her own face a mask.

"I couldn't possibly," she said. "Not today."

"You could possibly." he told her coldly. "Today

and every other day. One doesn't let small distractions enter into something like this, Christa."

Small distractions.

As she took her place in front of the keyboard, she thought it would have been much kinder of him to have simply slapped her in the face!

Ted Bentley came back from New York the Friday before Christmas, and his lack of surprise at finding Christa and Paul at work in the drawing room made her realize that the two men must have discussed Paul's plans for her by phone.

She knew, though, that Ted, like Honora, would approve of anything that would divert Paul, and she felt more than ever as if she were being used as a therapeutic pawn.

At dinner that night, Honora announced that she had decided to have a Christmas tree, for the first time in years.

It would be a huge tree, she proclaimed, and would be set up in the corner of the drawing room opposite the piano.

"We have scads of gorgeous old ornaments packed away in boxes in the attic," she said, unveiling her plans like an excited young girl, for when Honora was in a euphoric mood she went all the way with it. "Martha and Fitch and I are going to make a survey over the weekend, so we can fill in with anything else we may need. When I was a child, we always put up the tree Christmas Eve and stashed our presents under it, but we didn't open the presents until Christmas Day. Shall we follow that idea?"

Paul and Ted agreed, but Christa didn't bother to comment, for she didn't feel involved in this, although she was certain that Honora was going to ask her for Christmas dinner. But for the fact that Christmas was on a weekday she would have asked for time off, so that she could have escaped the Talbot house, probably by going to Boston.

As it was, she knew that even if Honora were willing to give her a brief vacation, Paul would be furious if their schedule were interrupted for more than a day or so.

Now, on this Friday night before Christmas, Ted, newly arrived on the scene, suggested that he drive Christa to Birch Street, but Paul swiftly vetoed the idea.

For a moment, Ted looked his annoyance. Then he smiled, and said, "Well, I suppose we'll have to defer to the professor, Christa."

She smiled back, but Paul did not seem to find the interchange at all amusing and he barely spoke to her as he drove her home.

As he pulled up in front of the music school, she said, "If you don't mind, I'd rather we don't have a lesson tomorrow morning," for he had insisted that they include Saturday mornings in the schedule, usually taking her back to Birch Street directly after lunch.

"Why?" he demanded bluntly.

"Christmas is just a few days away, and I *do* have some shopping to do," she said. "I've one gift which must be mailed to Boston. . . ."

"Is there someone in Boston?" Paul queried. "Who? A boyfriend?"

"No," Christa said, and wondered why he made her feel so defensive, as if she really owed him an explanation. "Glenda, the girl I went to secretarial school with in Albany. She actually got me the job in Boston, and we shared an apartment together."

"I see," he said. "Well, take the day then, if you must, only be careful driving around town. The weather forecast predicts snow. And be sure you practice two hours in the evening."

"I'll be sure," Christa promised him dully.

It seemed strange the next morning not to be getting ready for either Paul or Fitch to pick her up, and Christa lingered in the kitchen over a second cup of coffee, making out a tentative list and feeling her sense of holiday spirit increasing as she tried to decide what might be right for each person on it.

She wanted to get something special for Honora, but Honora was one of those "people who have everything." It would have to be a gift perfectly suited to her, something Christa hoped she would have the good fortune to stumble upon, for it could not be calculated in advance.

She decided that she would give Fitch a large tin of his favorite pipe tobacco, and she just might dare to buy him a pipe to go with it, even though she knew that this was an especially personal sort of thing with men who favored pipes. She decided upon a large box of chocolates for Martha, even though Martha surely didn't need the calories! But Martha loved sweets, and she was always cooking for other people. She would also get Martha something frivolous, maybe even a pretty, ruffly Christmas handkerchief with some sachets to go with it.

There must be a present for Ted too, of course, but she knew that she must take care not to make this gift too personal. Perhaps a set of shaving lotion and soap, in a scent other than the one Paul used, would be the safest choice, and she marked this tentatively on her list.

This brought her to Paul, and here she was totally stymied. She wished so very much that she might find something for him that would be a real memento; something that he would, perhaps, still keep and look at occasionally long after she had gone out of his life, and which would remind him of her.

She smiled at this kind of vanity. What could she possibly give Paul that would be an eternal reminder? She could think of nothing suitable for him at all.

No—she would have to stumble upon something for Paul even as she would for Honora.

The perfect present, insofar as Honora was concerned, was located in an exclusive little boutique that carried a small but exquisite selection of gifts.

There, nestled among a number of other lovely trinkets, Christa saw a tapestry-covered music box that simply *looked* like Honora. And, almost as if it had been ordained, the selection it played was the *Habanera* from "Carmen," one of the arias in which Honora had triumphed many times.

Christa quailed slightly after asking the price, knowing that the purchase would put a real dent in her budget, for she had convinced Honora that she must take a salary cut, though Honora had refused to make it as large a one as Christa felt it should be. Still, there was no question about buying the music box. She could not possibly hope to find anything else so appropriate.

She stashed Honora's gift at the bottom of a big Christmas-decorated shopping bag, and went on along the street feeling, increasingly, that special kind of glow that only Christmas can bring.

Everything else on her list fell into place, too. She bought the tobacco for Fitch and found a pipe she was sure he would like. She found some pretty amethyst earrings to be sent to Glenda, especially appropriate because Glenda's birthday was in February, and so amethysts were her birthstones.

She bought a magnificently lavish box of candy for Martha, plus a fluffy handkerchief embroidered with vivid poinsettias, and some fragrant sachets tied with pastel ribbons and ornamented with small, delicately executed flowers. She opted for a small traveling kit with an assortment of shaving aids for Ted, smelled carefully, and knew very definitely that this was *not* Paul's brand.

She paused in an ice cream shop that dated back to her high school days and splurged on a club sandwich and a chocolate soda for lunch, realizing as she ate that she *still* had absolutely no idea of what to get Paul.

The afternoon was waning as she explored from shop to shop, until finally she became convinced that she simply was not going to come across something as perfect for Paul as the music box was for Honora.

She was at a complete loss by the time she passed a shop where records, sheet music and a variety of small instruments were sold, which she had already passed at least a dozen times during the course of her foray. Now, though, she paused to look long and hard at a display that had been arranged in one corner, consisting, among other things of special lined paper designed for musical composition.

Her thoughts plunged back to the haunting theme Paul had been playing while he waited for her the other afternoon, the melody that he had dismissed lightly, when she asked him about it, as "nothing in particular."

In the interim, she realized she had been humming it to herself over and over again; it was that arresting. And, although she had not thought consciously of this before, she felt certain, now, that the theme was of Paul's own creation.

She stared at the composition paper. With this paper, one could write a song, or a sonata—or even a symphony, and she had a deep, though sudden, feeling that Paul had yet another talent in his repertory, and that he was, in fact, capable of doing any or all of these things.

She drew a deep breath. Would she *dare* give him composition materials as a Christmas gift?

Would she be able to tell him, swiftly enough, that she *knew* the theme he had been playing was *his*, and that she also knew it was good, for she had not been able to get it out of her mind?

Before she had a chance to think further on it, she opened the shop door, went inside, and, once home with her bag full of presents, it was the box intended for Paul that she wrapped first, using a blue paper sprinkled with silver stars, fastening shimmering silver ribbon around it, and ornamenting it further with a huge, shining bow.

Honora made a strong case for Christa to come out and stay overnight Christmas Eve in the lakefront mansion so that they would all be together to trim the tree and then open their presents Christmas morning, but Christa managed to avoid this.

She compromised by agreeing to stay to dinner on Christmas Eve and to linger for the tree trimming, this not involving any great change in plans because Paul had not seen any reason whatsoever why they should not have their usual lesson on Christmas Eve.

He did agree, however, that they might stop early so that the Christmas tree could be brought into the drawing room and set up in place.

It was a giant balsam, almost touching the ceiling so that a ladder was necessary to reach the upper branches when it came time to first wire on the lights, place the star on top, and then start trimming. Ted took over the task of doing this. Fitch was getting rather old to perch on ladders, Christa realized, and wiring a tree, especially under such circumstances, required two strong hands.

Fitch brought a bowl of eggnog in, once the wiring was finished and the lights switched on, and he and Martha came to join the rest of them in a toast. Honora was her sparkling best; she and Ted kept up the major part of the conversation throughout what Martha termed a "Christmas Eve supper," since the main dinner, which was to feature roast goose, would come the next day.

Paul was quiet, and Christa imagined that the tree wiring had made him especially conscious of his handicap, as so many things must. She was afraid that he might start drinking again, as he had at Thanksgiving, but he didn't.

It was he, as a matter of fact, who put a series of

Christmas records on the stereo after dinner, and helped heap the presents under the tree.

Honora had made one change in her "traditional" planning. She and Martha, conferring, had decided on a middle of the day dinner, prefaced by a very special rum punch, and had agreed that this would be the time to open the gifts rather than getting up early in the morning to do so.

"I'm not *that* much of a child at heart," Honora said lightly, but Christa felt certain that the gift opening had been delayed to ensure her presence, and she could not help but notice that several of the brightly wrapped packages bore her name. It wasn't difficult, either, to guess that most of them were from Honora, for they were done in dazzling shades of fuchsia and purple, ornamented with bright gold bows.

It was nearly midnight when, after a final eggnog, Christa said that she must be getting home, and Ted smiling across at her, agreed. "Otherwise," he said, "you'll never give Santa a chance to come down the chimney."

He stood, stretching. "Mind if I come along?" he asked Paul, who had already risen, obviously prepared to drive Christa back to the music school.

Paul shrugged. "The Corvette wasn't built for three," he pointed out, but Ted was not to be daunted.

"We can take my car," he said cheerfully. "It has a nice, wide front seat."

Ted took the wheel and Christa was placed in the middle, terribly aware of Paul's disturbing presence at her side.

She shivered, and he promptly asked, "Cold?" and before she had a chance to answer he put his arm around her, drawing her close to him. She could feel his warmth, his chin brushed her forehead, and she wanted to lean back against him, she wanted to let herself become locked in the circle of his arms, she wished that there were some way to wave a magic wand and make Ted disappear, much as she liked Ted.

When they pulled up in front of the music school, Ted glanced at his watch and said, "One minute to midnight. That's close enough."

He bent and kissed her lightly on the lips. "Merry Christmas, beautiful," he told her.

She could *feel* Paul's displeasure, and she wondered whether or not he might say anything to Ted on the way back. There was a "Hands Off" sign on her, no doubt about that. Increasingly, Paul was regarding her as a "property" rather than a person. He did not want her diverted by interests other than music.

The crisp snow crunched under their feet as Paul walked across with her to the front door and waited until she had switched on the light in the vestibule. Then he lingered for a moment, looking down at her.

"I know Honora said to be ready at one o'clock tomorrow," he told her, "but would you make it half an hour or so earlier? I've a reason for asking."

He was speaking in such a low tone that his voice couldn't possibly carry to the curb, where Ted did have the front window turned down slightly.

Mystified, she said, "Of course," and he nodded slightly.

"Good night, then," he said, and before she had the chance to even think about whether or not *he* might proffer a Merry Christmas kiss he turned and headed back to the car.

It snowed again during the night, and Christa awoke to find the world outside her window a perfect Christmas card scene.

She put her coat and the shopping bag full of

presents on the chair in the vestibule, and she wondered as she did so why Paul had asked her to be ready early. What "reason" could he possibly have?

Last night, he had been annoyed at Ted's insistence that he come along too, when it was time to take her home. Was this because he had been prepared to tell her something that he didn't want to discuss in front of Ted or even Honora?

Had he possibly decided to "join the world" again and leave Lakeport after the holidays, which would mean an end to the lessons?

Christa went cold at the mere thought of this, and sat down abruptly in the nearest chair, actually trembling.

She had chosen a dress today of Christmas green that was cinched at the waist and full-skirted. She had brushed her hair into a golden cascade, and was wearing thin-strapped gold slippers, more suitable for evening, but this, after all, was a holiday.

She had taken great pains with her appearance, but now she didn't even want to glance in a mirror; she was sure that she had turned ashy.

True, she had known that eventually the lessons must come to an end, but regardless, they had become an increasingly vital part of her life.

In just the short time that she had been Paul's pupil she had made miraculous strides, even though sometimes he exhausted her. He could be brutal when he wanted her to achieve a certain effect with her music, he was extremely demanding, his ear was unfailingly accurate and his sense of timing so acute that she could not be "off" in her playing even a fraction of a beat without knowing that a heavy frown would be spreading across his face, even though she didn't dare to turn her head in his direction to see it.

He very seldom praised her, and yet there were times when she surprised an expression of satisfaction on his face and knew that she had pleased him, and at such moments she was inwardly exultant.

Now the thought that the lessons might come to an end as quickly as they had begun was almost more than she could bear, leaving her with such a sweeping sense of desolation that when she heard the doorbell ring she went to answer it with hesitant, almost dragging, steps.

Paul stood before her, and because she had been thinking so intently about the possibility that he might soon be going out of her life, she let herself look at him, *really* look at him, then wished she hadn't. His striking good looks were heightened, today, not only by the perfectly fitting tan leather coat he was wearing, which had a belt that emphasized his slim waist and, thus, his wide and muscular shoulders, but by a kind of glow that came, she told herself quickly, not from seeing *her* but from December's sting touching his cheeks with color.

He had carefully combed his thick, dark hair so that it intensified the perfect shape of his head, and his eyes were a clear and direct gray. She tried not to let her own eyes linger on his mouth, on the full, generous lips which, even in repose, gave a promise of the kind of sensuality she had experienced at first hand, but it was hard not to do so.

He looked down at her and laughed, his features lighting in a singularly carefree smile.

"What is this—inspection?" he asked her.

"I—I'm sorry," she stammered, and held the door open wide. "Come in, won't you."

Automatically, she led the way into the studio. She had not bothered to light a fire, knowing that she soon would be going out, but she *had* turned up the thermostat a notch or two. Still, the room was chilly, which gave her an excuse for a shiver which actually had a lot more to do with Paul than it did with the temperature.

She sat down, waiting for him to sit down too and say whatever it was he wished to say to her, but he merely stood, as if waiting for *her*, until she said, "Well?"

"Get up, will you?" he asked her.

She did so, puzzled, and he said, his lips twisting in a teasing sort of smile, "Do you suppose you could come a bit closer?"

She approached him warily, and he grinned. "Honestly, Christa," he told her, "I'm not about to bite you! This isn't lesson time!"

So he was aware, then, of what a bear he could be when he was teaching her!

"Look," he said, "stop shirking away like a scared wren, will you? Actually," viewing her appraisingly, "you don't look like a wren at all, except on those rare occasions when you persist in pinning your hair up in that hideous bun or knot or whatever you call it. You are—very lovely today."

He opened his coat, and pointed. "I've gone in for Christmas colors myself," he said, showing her a glimpse of a bright red vest. "And wait till you see Ted! He's wearing a coat that must have been left over from St. Patrick's Day." The gray eyes darkened just a shade, and he reached into his coat pocket. "I would have given this to you last night if Ted hadn't tagged along with us," he said. "I wanted to give it to you privately, though it's not all that much. But I'm not too fond of making public offerings."

He handed her a small box, and she took it from him, her fingers cold.

"Open it," he urged her, and she did so, carefully undoing the pretty silver and green ribbon.

She lifted the lid to encounter a square of cotton. Removing that, she saw a small, gold grand piano, suspended from a slender chain.

Both its beauty—and its significance—touched her

so deeply that her eyes were shimmering with tears as she looked up at Paul, and he said softly, "Here, put it on. I'll help you."

He took the necklace from her, and fumbled awkwardly with the clasp, trying to do with his right hand, principally, what was really a two-hand job.

His mouth tightened, and she yearned to simply take the necklace away from him and put it on herself, but she had the good sense to stand quietly, waiting for him.

At last he managed to open the clasp, and he looked down at her, his smile rueful. "Lord, but I'm clumsy!" he said. "Turn around, will you, and let's see if I can get this around your neck without choking you?"

She obliged, and then felt his fingers upon her skin, and his touch electrified her. Her body began emitting impulses which she *knew* she must suppress, but when, finally, he fastened the clasp, it was all she could do not to turn to him, not to put her arms around him and draw his beloved, dark head down close to her, so that she could reach his mouth.

It was he, however, who turned her around with gentle fingers. His eyes lingered on the tiny piano, lying against her creamy throat, and they moved downward, encompassing the swell of her breasts, and the smallness of her waistline, then continuing to the curve of her hips, which the fabric of her dress seemed to reveal rather than conceal with its fullness.

His eyes darkened, but he said only, "The piano looks—very nice. I consider it—a kind of symbol. Keep it always, will you, Christa?"

She could not speak, she could only nod affirmatively. Then his lips found hers, but this was a gentle kiss, tender, loving. Yes, that *was* the word for it, she thought with astonishment, even as she responded to him.

Loving!

"Merry Christmas," he said, and now she made no attempt at camouflage, she let her adoration for him shine forth in her eyes.

But he was already turning away from her; he said, "We'd better get on our way. Honora will be angry if we're late."

Chapter Ten

Honora and Ted had already had their first cup of Christmas punch, and it seemed to have gone directly to their heads. Ted promptly stashed the presents Christa had brought beneath the breathtakingly beautiful tree, and seemed especially pleased when he noted that there was something for him among them.

The house had never looked lovelier. Each door was decorated with a holly wreath tied with enormous red velvet bows, white candles gleamed in every window, and, in addition to the tree, for decoration in the drawing room there was the focal point of a huge, exquisite Della Robbia wreath over the fireplace which, Honora said, had been given to her in Italy years ago, by a "secret admirer."

Honora, really beautiful today in a couturier gown of gleaming ruby satin, was thoroughly enjoying Christmas. This, she said, was the most marvelous Christmas she had known in "decades," due to the fact that she had three people of whom she was extremely fond around her. She insisted that they drink a toast to this.

Ted responded with a second toast which virtually eliminated Christa's first cup of punch, and Paul refilled it, and his own as well. At this point, Honora insisted that Ted fetch Martha and Fitch, so that the present opening ceremony could begin, this to precede dinner—and as Christa's eyes strayed to the large package under the tree wrapped in star-spattered blue paper, she knew in a horrible moment that she had done entirely the wrong thing.

Paul had given her the little gold piano privately. He had said that he was not fond of public offerings, yet with her gift she was making not merely an offering but a downright blatant suggestion toward what he could attempt to do with the balance of his life!

She should have expressed her feelings about his potential as a composer under entirely different circumstances, she knew now, and was horrified at her audacity in even *thinking* of giving him such a gift in front of all the others.

She waited in a state of chilled apprehension, as present after present was opened, one at a time.

Honora had brought her a beautiful cream velvet tunic, and a silken caftan of a blue that almost exactly matched her eyes, with exotic little velvet embroidered harem slippers of the same shade to go with it. Ted had brought her a bottle of perfume from New York. Martha had crocheted a lacy mo-hair scarf for her, and Fitch proffered a copper pot in which he had planted narcissus bulbs that, he told her, would soon start to bloom, to become a harbinger of spring.

She managed the proper exclamations about her presents, and Fitch, Martha and Ted were equally delighted with theirs, while Honora went into raptures about the music box, insisting upon playing it for all of them and even singing a few bars of the *Habanera* in her still-magnificent soprano voice.

It seemed as if the moment would never come for Ted to hand Paul the blue-starred box, and Christa wished, desperately, that somehow it could just vanish through the floor.

But finally Paul was unwrapping it, and as she held her breath he stared down at the contents.

She could not quite believe the range of expressions that crossed his face. Incredulity merged with disbelief, yielding to a towering kind of rage that kindled his eyes and instinctively made her shrink away from him.

Honora, still toying with the music box, glanced up idly, noting only that he was taking considerable time in commenting on the gift, which she knew had come from Christa.

"Well, Paul," she said lightly, "are you leaving us in suspense, or are you going to tell us what Christa has given you?"

He glanced coldly across at his aunt, the rage having faded so that now his gray eyes were purely glacial, and he looked like a man carved from stone.

He said, "I doubt I'd want to share this with anyone. There's only one place for it."

His eyes bored into Christa's, and she shrank from the absolute hatred she saw in them.

He said, "You could have saved yourself a bit of money by simply buying me one of those rubber pacifiers, like they stick in babies' mouths."

Then, as she watched helplessly, he took the box and its contents, the wrappings, even the silver bow that she had lavished such loving care upon, and before anyone could check him he walked over to the fireplace, pushed aside the screen, and threw the whole thing into the blazing flames.

For a breathless moment he stood, statuelike, gazing down as papers and ribbons curled to become charred ruins. Then, without a further word to anyone, he stalked out of the room and they could hear his footsteps retreating up the staircase.

The stillness that followed his departure was intense. In it, the sound of the crackling fire echoed like a battle being fought in full scale.

Finally, Honora found her voice and she said with obvious effort, "Christa, my dear, I am so *sorry!*"

Ted was frowning. "What did you *give* him?" he demanded. "He didn't give the rest of us a chance to even get a glimpse of it."

Martha and Fitch had moved close together, they were looking at her with unconcealed sympathy.

Her eyes roved, miserably, from one to another of the four persons in the room with her, and she said, "It was something I thought would be very—*right*. Now I know I was being exceedingly stupid."

"Christa," Honora was beginning to get control of herself again, "I think we all know that you would never do anything to deliberately hurt Paul, so don't look so—stricken. We know you love him as much as we do. . . ."

Her words trailed off, but her eyes met Christa's directly, nor did Christa flinch from them.

Yes, she loved Paul. She loved him totally, but hers was the most lost of causes; she had never deceived herself about that.

Now she asked herself how she could ever face him again? And the answer came that she *must,* and that she must face him *now*.

Honora said, "Martha, can you hold dinner? I hate to ask it of you, but I *would* like to wait till Paul comes back down."

Martha nodded, although not too happily, for she was especially particular about her wonderfully prepared food being served at precisely the proper time.

Honora added, "Fitch, open some champagne, will you? We've had enough punch, I think, and I'm not sure champagne is a good follow-up, but I think we all need something."

As Fitch nodded and quietly left the room, Ted said, "I'd give you odds that Paul won't come down again."

"He must," Honora said sharply. "This *is* Christmas!"

With this, Christa stood up and swallowed hard. "I'm going after him," she announced, then left the room so quickly neither Honora nor Ted had a chance to make a comment.

Once at the top of the stairs, though, her temporary rush of courage faltered. She stood staring down the long hallway which ran both to the right and the left of her. Honora's bedroom and boudoir were to the right. Paul's room, she knew, was to the left, directly next door to the room where she had stayed back in October, after her Uncle Julian had died.

The hall was thickly carpeted; her gold slippers made no sound as she walked along slowly, coming to a stop, finally, in front of the door which, she knew, had been closed with the firm intent of blocking out everyone.

She realized that her only possible choice of action was to simply open the door and go in, for the chance was much too strong that if she knocked and identified herself Paul would not admit her.

He could, of course, have locked the door, and if this proved to be so she would *have* to call out to him. But, when she tried the knob, it turned.

The only light in the room was the white Christmas candle shining in the window, but it cast a glow across the bed accentuating the shape of Paul's long figure. He was lying face down, and he did not so much as stir as she went to him.

She sat down on the side of the bed, reaching out tentatively to touch his raven hair, to stroke it, as she had wished to do so many, many times.

For a long moment he remained entirely still; then he turned over with an abruptness that startled her.

There was such venom in his glance, evident even in this dim light, that she shrank back from him as if she had been stung.

His eyes were twin abysses, and his lips twisted in

a snarl. "What were you trying to do?" he asked her thickly. "Why *didn't* you buy me a rubber pacifier—or a miniature crutch?"

Christa summoned every ounce of reserve strength she possessed, and met his gaze directly. She said steadily, "Because you don't need either!"

"What is that supposed to mean?"

"Will you listen if I tell you?" she asked him, her heart throbbing wildly beneath her carefully controlled outward calm.

He pushed bedpillows behind his head, propped himself up on them, and Christa was acutely aware of the outlines of his long body, just a touch away from her own hands.

She tried to force her thoughts away from this disturbing knowledge of his physical nearness. She said, knowing that she would get nowhere with him unless she was bold, "I've realized all along that you've been putting up a front which I admire very much. I didn't realize though, that underneath it you've actually been feeling desperately sorry for yourself."

She heard his quick intake of breath, she would not have been surprised if he had slapped her. But after another long moment he said only, "Go on."

"I think," she said, "that if a person has a God given talent they have an obligation to use it."

"You're a great one to talk!" he sneered. "You were in the process of throwing your own God given talent away when I met you."

She drew a long breath. "Only because I didn't recognize it," she said, "and I *still* think you exaggerate it."

"Then you're even more of a fool than I've sometimes thought you were!"

This stung. She yearned to retaliate with an equally caustic remark, and yet she knew that it was vital she retain her own composure. She must not let him provoke her to anger or her chance would be lost; and, once lost, it might never again be regained.

She said quietly, "For the moment, could we leave me out of it and concentrate on *you?* Obviously, I can't make the same initial judgment about you. You used your talent as a pianist to its maximum. . . ."

"Not quite," he interrupted. "You've always had the problem of looking at me—as a concert artist, at least—through some kind of mental glasses that have very distorted lenses. I had *not* reached my zenith, Christa. I had a way to go. In my opinion, any artist *always* has a way to go. When the day comes that they dispute this, you can be sure they are past their prime."

"All right," she said. "I'll agree to that. Nevertheless, you did *use* your first talent. I went about it in a very bumbling way today, but what I was asking of you is that you use your *second* talent to equal effectiveness."

He stared at her. "Just what *are* you getting at?" he demanded, but although there was anger in his tone it was diminished, and she knew, elatedly, that she had succeeded in capturing his interest.

"I think that you could be as great a composer as you were a pianist," she said staunchly. "Maybe greater."

She very nearly weakened when she heard the scoffing tone of his laughter.

"You're out of your mind!" he accused her.

"On the contrary," she said, sitting up straight and now very sure of herself, "I'm *right*. I know I'm right. I think I knew it the first time I heard you playing that theme on the piano, and later realized it was yours. I couldn't get the theme out of my mind—I still haven't been *able* to get it out of my mind, nor can you get it out of yours. You may not realize it, but you keep whistling it. . . ."

"I keep *whistling* it?" he asked incredulously.

"Often," she said. "Especially when we go for our walks along the lake."

"And you think," he was sardonic now, "that because I happened to latch onto a catchy theme I'm capable of becoming another Beethoven or Bach or God knows who?"

"I think you're capable of becoming Paul Talbot," she said quietly, "and I think that will be quite enough."

He reached out and switched on a bedside lamp by way of answer, and she had never before felt so revealed as she did by its aura of light.

He said, contemplatively, "You're beautiful. It seems to me that you've consistently become more beautiful lately, that you've been blossoming out, to be very cliché about it, both as an artist and a woman. It's an enticing and extremely disturbing combination, Christa, yet I don't think you're even aware of it. It's no wonder that Ted is so crazy about you. I imagine that even when you were playing the part of the little wren you left a lot of men behind you wherever you went who—wanted you. You must face up to the fact that from here on you shall have to literally fight them off."

"Don't be ridiculous!" she chided him.

"Ah, but I'm not being ridiculous. Can't you guess what I'd like to do right at this moment with you?"

She could guess. She could not only guess, but she knew that were he to attempt to do what he wanted to do she would be totally unable to deny him, for her own body would prove to be a traitor capable of infinite treachery.

He said, his eyes lighting, "I can see that you *do* know. But where does that put me? If I were to possess you, Christa, it would have to include every last fiber of your being, do you understand that? There would not be a particle of you, either physical or emotional or mental, that I would not want to capture and conquer. It would have to be a total giving, and afterward everything would never again be the same between us, do you understand that?"

She faltered, but she said, "Yes. Yes, I do."

"Have you given anything of yourself to a man, Christa?"

Only to you, she wanted to tell him. Whatever there has been of any significance at all has been only to you. No one else has ever really touched me.

Her throat seemed to close, though, when it came to voicing such words to him, but he only smiled in a rueful way, then he said, a thickness to his voice, "You don't have to answer me. I realized when I first met you that you're a virgin. I realized subsequently that my role was to be your teacher, not the lover who awakens you, and there is no way of my playing a dual part. If I were to take you now, Christa," and as he spoke he reached out his hand, outlining with it the curve of her breasts beneath the folds of green material, "you would not come back tomorrow and sit down at the piano and do the things you must do. You speak of God given talent. Start to recognize your *own* talent, little one. This isn't caprice on my part, teaching you. It's because I know where you *belong*, do you understand that?"

She could not answer this, because she knew that any reply she could make would only be negative.

She loved music, there was no doubt of that. She had always loved it and she had had dreams that had died hard, but they *had* died. Even though Paul had reawakened in her all of the desire she had ever felt to *play*, he had not succeeded in reviving those dreams, nor did she intend to permit them to become revived. She no longer could tolerate visions of Christa Emery standing on a concert stage, receiving great bouquets and bowing as the audience applauded wildly.

He was watching her closely and finally he seemed to come to a conclusion of his own.

He said, as if he were speaking to a child, "Run along downstairs. I'll be with you in a few minutes."

She stood, resenting this treatment, but once again he disarmed her.

He said, smiling a crooked smile that twisted her heart, "I apologize, Christa, for doing what I did with your gift. I admit that my immediate reaction led only to fury, and once again I behaved like the worst kind of clod. But, regardless, I appreciate what you were trying to do. Even though I destroyed your present, I still thank you for it."

Before joining the others downstairs Christa paused in Honora's boudoir to stare, for a moment, at her mirrored reflection, while she tried to get her own surging and conflicting emotions under control.

Thus, when she reached the drawing room again, Paul arrived almost on her heels, and Honora at once proffered champagne for both of them.

Coffee and liqueurs were served in the drawing room after dinner. But before Christa had a chance to taste her coffee Paul looked across at her and said lazily, "I've been thinking it's time my pupil makes her debut. Play something for us, Christa!"

It was a command, not a request. Even Honora noticed this, Christa saw, and the older woman frowned and seemed about to speak.

Christa was sure that just a moment before she had heard a telephone ringing, however, and she was right; Fitch appeared in the doorway.

"It's for you, Mr. Paul," he said, adding, almost coldly, "Miss De Platte is calling from New York."

Gloria De Platte's Christmas call had saved her, in a sense, Christa realized, but this did not make her any happier about it.

Paul rose quickly enough to go and answer the phone, telling Fitch that he would take the call in the library, nor did he seem especially surprised by it.

They had surely been in touch with each other before now, this was absolutely evident, Christa told herself miserably, or his reaction would have been quite different.

She drank her liqueur without even realizing it, and Ted came across the room to fill her glass. He seemed to accept the call casually, too, it was only Honora who appeared vexed.

"Give me some more Benedictine, will you please, Ted," she asked, her eyebrows creasing in a frown. "That woman . . ."

"You wouldn't expect Gloria to forget Christmas, would you?" Ted asked lightly.

"I don't know *what* I would expect her to do," Honora admitted, then made what was clearly a deliberate switch of subject. "Do you feel like playing for us, Christa?"

"I'd rather not, tonight," Christa said frankly. "After all that dinner . . ." she added lamely.

Honora nodded understandingly. "Then we won't press you," she said. "And you really mustn't let Paul bully you so. . . ."

"I think he only wants to show her off," Ted interjected, and his eyes lingered upon her, too caressing for comfort. "You can hardly blame him for that," he added softly.

He tried to lead the conversation into varied channels, to draw Honora out about her book, and both Honora and Christa were polite enough to follow his lead. Nevertheless, Christa was conscious of the fact that Honora was disturbed by Gloria De Platte's call. She had long since gotten the impression that Honora didn't like her nephew's fiancée— but, actually, *was* Gloria still Paul's fiancée?

Had theirs been one of those situations where she had brought the engagement to an end, after the accident? Had it been Paul, the concert star, about whom she had really cared, rather than Paul the man?

Christa wished that she could come right out and *ask,* and then realized that a major reason why she didn't was because she was afraid of the answer she might get.

When Paul returned he was actually humming the theme that haunted her so, as he crossed the foyer and came into the drawing room. He caught her eye as he ended the tune, and she glimpsed what she would only have termed deviltry, had this been anyone other than Paul.

As he poured himself a liqueur, he turned to Ted and said, "I hope you haven't tied yourself up with anything for New Year's Eve."

"No," Ted said, "I haven't. I assumed we'd spend it here."

"Gloria's family is throwing quite a bash, and she wants us both to come." Paul said. He sipped his liqueur, then smiled a smile so tantalizing that Christa could barely resist the urge to personally wipe it off his face.

"I think it's about time I came out of the woods, don't you?" he asked, of the room at large.

Paul and Ted left for New York early New Year's Eve morning, they were gone by the time Christa presented herself at the house, as usual, to work with Honora, but Honora was in no mood today to continue with her book.

"I can't abide the thought of Paul going back to that woman!" she said, as she and Christa drank coffee together.

"Going back to her?" Christa questioned.

"Well—continuing on with her, doing whatever you want to call it," Honora amended. "I've only met her two or three times, Paul has never brought her here. I suppose I've made it rather clear that I wasn't about to issue an invitation to her. True, she *certainly* isn't after him for his money. Paul has enough, but her family could buy and sell him. I thought, personally, that it was his fame that attracted her, the thought of sharing the spotlight with him. I rather imagined it was over between them, as a matter of fact. Neither he nor Ted has mentioned her since he came here. But now she merely telephones, and he simply *leaps* to her side. . . .''

Honora made a consummately dramatic gesture that might have been amusing under any other circumstances, but was not in the least so now.

"Darling," she said, "there is just no *point* in my trying to do anything today, and you shouldn't be working on New Year's Eve anyway. I hope you have some interesting plans of your own for tonight."

Honora didn't realize how few people she had contacted in Lakeport since her return, Christa knew, nor was she about to tell her now. The few old school friends who remained in town were married, some already had children. Some had phoned her, and issued invitations which she had declined, supposedly because of her job, but the truth was that over these weeks since she had been working with both Honora and Paul she had had neither the time nor energy for anything more.

Her next door neighbors, the Andersons, *had* asked her over to "see in" the New Year. She knew that Honora had accepted an invitation from friends of long standing for dinner and the evening at their home, but would insist that she come too if she left the impression she might be at loose ends. So she said, forcing a smile, "Well, I *am* going to a small party . . ."

"Good!" Honora said briskly, and added, cryptically, "When midnight comes, drink a toast to Paul's coming to his senses, will you?"

Christa awoke to a New Year's morning that was a dull morning at best. Snow threatened, and she thought with nostalgia of the winter holiday time when she had been a child, first with her parents, then later with Faith and Julian.

It had been a season filled with excitement and fun, and snow had been one of the best parts of it. She remembered sledding with her friends up on the hill back of the old cemetery, and making snow ice cream with her Aunt Faith, assiduously stirring sugar and vanilla and cream into a bowl of freshly gathered snow to make an unsurpassed concoction. She remembered participating vigorously in snowball fights out on the schoolyard, and sometimes lying down in freshly fallen snow to make "angel" patterns by thrusting out eager arms and legs into a partial circle.

Some afternoons when she and Paul had walked along the lakefront it had begun to snow, and there had been a sense of childhood joy in sharing the fresh, clean tang of the frosty air with him. Once he actually had picked up a scoop of snow and tossed a ball at her, holding her off when she had come charging at him, ready to retaliate.

They had built up a camaraderie during those pre-lesson walks sometimes lost in the course of the lessons themselves. Would they recapture it, once the lessons resumed again, *if* the lessons resumed again?

Christa wondered about this.

Matters were soon to take their own course. She was just beginning to run water for a bath when the phone rang. It was Honora. "I called to say Happy New Year, darling," she began, but there was something in her voice that made Christa instantly sure she had a lot more to say than that.

"Paul telephoned a few minutes ago," Honora said.

"Oh?"

"He wanted to tell me that he will be staying in

New York for several days, so there won't be any lessons until some time next week," Honora went on, and then her voice grew cold. "He wants to bring Gloria De Platte back here with him when he returns," she finished.

Christa felt as if she had suddenly swallowed a giant ice cube. Her throat was so constricted that she could not make an immediate reply and finally Honora asked, anxiously, "Christa, are you still there?"

"Yes," Christa said, but it was a faint affirmative.

"Christa." Honora herself sounded at the edge of desperation. "I fully realized it Christmas Day. You love him, don't you?"

"Please, Honora . . ."

"Child, if you will confide in me, you may be sure that I will never breach your confidence. Actually, I think I've known it for quite a while. I've watched you look at him when you were sure he wouldn't notice. But, conversely, I've watched him watching *you*. I know the signs. I would swear that he's also fallen in love with you. That's why I can't understand . . ."

Christa interrupted. "He isn't in the least in love with me, Honora. I'm his current project, that's all. He has convinced himself that he can wave a magic wand and put me on the concert stage in his place. It's all wrong, and I've *felt* it was all wrong, right from the beginning. Now . . ."

"I think you're mistaken, Christa," Honora interrupted. "Paul would never toy with talent, believe me. He wouldn't be encouraging you as he is if he didn't feel that you really *do* have that certain something that's essential for an artist to succeed. You must believe that, Christa!"

Christa sighed. Honora, she realized, adored Paul, and in many ways she was blinded because of this adoration.

"Christa," Honora said now, anxiously, "come out here, will you? I know it's a holiday, I don't want you to come to work, of course, merely to talk. I think there are a number of things you and I should talk about."

Christa said swiftly, "I'm afraid I've made other plans."

"I'm glad," Honora said decisively. "Perhaps you can stop by later, though. Fitch can take you home."

"I don't know," Christa said, "I don't want to promise."

She was deliberately vague, and they left it at that, although she knew that Honora was not satisfied and would undoubtedly be ringing again before the day was over.

She went back to finish running her bath, but again the telephone pealed, and this time it truly seemed as if fate were taking a firm hand in the molding of her life.

Glenda bubbled a Happy New Year at the other end of the line, and then announced jubilantly that she was calling from her parents' home which, Christa remembered from their days in secretarial school together, was a spacious colonial house on the outskirts of Albany.

"I'm back to stay," Glenda reported happily. "I just wasn't happy in Boston after you left, and when a friend of my father's offered me this fantastic job in *his* law firm, I decided it would be idiotic to turn it down. I wish you weren't so tied up in Lakeport, Christa. He needs another girl and the pay is not half bad. My parents have a wing we're fixing up as an apartment. We could share it, and the cost would be nominal. . . ."

To her own astonishment, Christa found herself saying levelly, "I'm not tied up in Lakeport, Glenda. Not any more. This is—well, it's so coincidental you won't believe it! I can leave immediately, or almost immediately, if tonight wouldn't be too soon for me to come."

"Tonight!" Glenda shrieked. "That's too good to be true!"

"I think I can get there before long," Christa said, speaking swiftly before she could even start to think and, just possibly, change her mind.

Chapter Eleven

The Murrays' house was blazing with light when the taxi pulled up in front of it, and despite the snow that was falling Glenda came running out the door within seconds to envelop Christa in a bear hug.

The Murrays welcomed her warmly. They were in their late fifties, a comfortable couple with whom Christa had always felt at home, and although they might have wondered at her sudden impulse to leave Lakeport they were not overly inquisitive, for which she was grateful.

With Glenda, however, it was something else again. Glenda was brimming with curiosity.

There was one bedroom yet to be painted in the apartment wing, which was just as well, Glenda pointed out, because it meant Christa could choose her own color scheme. Since there were twin beds in her own room, however, accommodations in the interim posed no problem.

Christa unpacked only the things she would need for the night, while Glenda watched her, and Glenda was sharp. She said suddenly, "You've changed, Chris. You've become downright beautiful, for one thing, and please don't try to deny to me that there's been a man involved in all of this. I know this famous singer you've been working for must have all sorts of glamour tricks at her fingertips, but that isn't the answer."

Glenda waited, expectantly, and when Christa didn't reply, she was visibly disappointed, but she said generously, "If you really don't want to talk about it, Chris, I'll understand."

"I *do* want to talk about it," Christa found herself saying slowly—and the strange part of it was that she did.

She needed to pour out everything about Paul and her music and Honora and Ted and Gloria De Platte and all the rest of it, to someone who was a real friend. As she talked, the minutes stretched into an hour and she still continued while Glenda, her piquant face unaccustomedly serious, listened intently.

When she was done, finally, she leaned back against the pillows with a sigh close to exhaustion, admittedly ready for sympathy; but Glenda merely frowned.

"Had I known all of this," she said finally, "I wouldn't have phoned you this morning!"

Christa stared at her, shocked. "How can you say that?"

"What do you *expect* me to say?" her friend countered. "That I think you did the right thing? Well, I don't!"

Christa closed her eyes, too weary to pursue it, but Glenda was not about to let up on her, not yet.

"I remember when you went to Paul Talbot's concert in Boston last year," she told Christa. "You came home walking on some sort of a celestial ladder. I could see moon dust in your hair."

"You might better say in my eyes," Christa retorted cynically. "I was a stage struck little fool, I know that now. It had been Paul, all my life; ever since I was old enough to—to fantasize romance, that is."

"And it is *still* Paul, isn't it?" Glenda asked.

"That no longer matters," Christa evaded. "Don't you *see*—I'm just a *symbol* to him!"

"What makes you so sure of that?"

Christa moaned, "Everything! Do I need to spell it out again, Glenda? I've told you the whole sorry story!"

Glenda nodded sagely. "Hang in there, darling," she advised lightly. "I'm about to go and swipe some of dad's best brandy."

She left the room, and for a moment Christa stared at her surroundings, recognizing some of the bric-a-brac Glenda had had in their Boston apartment.

It had done her good to talk things out with a friend, Christa was more than willing to concede that, but it was disturbing to think that Glenda had come to the conclusion that she had done the wrong thing in leaving Lakeport.

When she came back with the brandy, Glenda obviously had been doing further thinking, for she asked, "How can you be so sure Paul really intends to marry this De Platte woman? Did he ever say they were engaged?"

"No, it never came up. He only mentioned her to me once, as a matter of fact. . . ."

Her cheeks burned when she remembered Paul's suggestion that he had a friend who could teach her things she needed to know about the art of dressing and of makeup. Still, she had to admit that it was at that point that she had begun to pay real attention to her appearance, taking pains with the clothes she chose to wear to the lakefront house, and, generally speaking, avoiding the bun that always provoked such a negative reaction from Paul.

She sighed, and Glenda said firmly, "Come on, doll. Drink up that brandy, and then I'm putting out the lights. You've had more than enough on your plate for one day. Let's hold off on anything else until tomorrow!"

Christa slept a sleep of pure exhaustion New Year's night, awakening the next morning to find that Glenda had already gone to work, leaving a note pinned to her bed pillow which stated simply, "Rest! The shadows under your eyes last night were two feet long!"

She smiled as she read the note, contemplated getting up, but, instead, rolled over on her side and promptly went back to sleep.

She awakened to find that it was snowing again, and she went to the window to look out upon a typically suburban scene. This was a new area of carefully planned development homes, spaced on fairly large lots, and the houses were attractive; but there was a similarity about them that Christa didn't care for, personally.

She shrugged into a pretty yellow corduroy housecoat, hoping the color would make her seem brighter than she felt. She was still weary, despite sleeping so late—for, looking at her watch, she saw to her surprise that it was after ten—and still disturbed by Glenda's conviction that she had left Lakeport too hastily.

Nevertheless, she told herself, as she brushed her hair, then decided to dispense with any makeup for the present, Glenda was overlooking the principal ingredient in her decision which, of course, was Paul.

Thinking about his quick response to Gloria De Platte's phone call, she knew that she could not possibly have done otherwise.

Mrs. Murray insisted on fixing a late breakfast of French toast and crisp bacon for Christa, then sat down at the breakfast nook in the kitchen, pouring coffee for both of them, with every intention of "keeping Christa company" while she ate.

She almost immediately turned the conversation to Honora Brent, whom she had seen perform at New York's Metropolitan Opera years before. She wanted to know all about Honora, and this was a request Christa found easy enough to oblige, even doing so with enthusiasm.

It was only Paul she didn't want to talk about.

Breakfast over, she joined Mrs. Murray for a time in front of the television set, but she knew nothing of the story line involved in the daytime dramas Glenda's mother enjoyed, and it was difficult to repress her restlessness.

Glenda called just before noon to report, ruefully, that she had hoped to get the afternoon off but it was going to be impossible, because on this day, of all days, her employer had scheduled a major legal conference and really needed her.

He had promised, however, that she could have all of tomorrow free, Glenda said, and he hoped that in the course of it she would bring Christa by and introduce her.

"You'll have no trouble at all getting a job here," Glenda said.

It was still snowing, but in any event the outdoors did not tempt her for she felt very, very tired. After a late lunch of soup and delicious hot rolls, she was more than willing to fall in with Mrs. Murray's suggestion that she go upstairs and "lie down with a book," and perhaps take a little nap. By then, Mrs. Murray said Glenda would probably be on her way home; with the weather the way it was she imagined the lawyers would not linger over their business any longer than strictly necessary.

The bed *was* inviting. Christa had found a novel downstairs that looked interesting and now she curled up with it, but very soon the pages blurred, and she could feel herself dozing off.

To her surprise, it was dark outside when she awakened. She glanced at the illuminated dial on the bedside clock and saw that it was nearly five-thirty. She was still in her yellow housecoat and, despite the fact that she seemed to have been sleeping the better part of the time since she had arrived at the Murray house, she remained as limp and exhausted as if she were convalescing from a long illness.

She decided to go downstairs and ask Mrs. Murray if she could make herself a cup of hot, strong, bracing tea. This she would bring back up with her while she dressed, and she determined that she would choose something especially colorful to wear, and take pains with her appearance; otherwise, Glenda would be all too sharp in guessing that Lakeport was still very much on her friend's mind!

Christa could hear water running in the kitchen sink as she approached the kitchen door, a pan rattled, and she realized Mrs. Murray was probably already starting dinner preparations. Then, to her dismay, she heard voices. Christa's mother must have a guest.

Briefly, she hesitated—but it was a man's tones she heard in counterpoint to Mrs. Murray's voice, so the natural assumption was that this was Glenda's father, back home from his office.

Christa had known him long enough so that she didn't in the least mind him seeing her in her housecoat while she made her tea. She stepped over the kitchen threshold, ready to say something light by way of greeting—only to find herself staring into Paul Talbot's blazingly angry eyes.

Mrs. Murray said, archly, "You have a visitor, Christa. I went upstairs to fetch you but you were fast asleep, and Mr. Talbot insisted I shouldn't wake you."

"No," Paul drawled. "I'd say she needs her beauty rest."

He smiled as he said it, but Christa at once

became acutely conscious of her tousled hair and her wan, weary looking face, and it was all she could do not to snap back at him.

Two could play his game, though, she decided determinedly, and she forced a smile and said, "How *considerate* of you, Paul. But what in the world are you doing here?"

"I had to drive to New York this morning," he said, and had she not seen the pure, metallic fury in his eyes she would have thought he was as pleasant a person as Mrs. Murray obviously assumed he was, for Glenda's mother was looking up at him with definitely admiring eyes. "The weather's miserable, but they're doing a pretty good job keeping the Thruway cleared. I thought it would be easier for you if I simply stopped by and took you back to Lakeport with me. It would be a dreary bus trip, under these conditions."

Mrs. Murray had put a kettle of water on the stove to boil, and Christa smelled the fragrance of something baking in the oven.

Now the kettle began to whistle, and Mrs. Murray transferred its contents to a capacious teapot, over which she placed an old-fashioned, crocheted "warmer."

"I always steep it," she told Paul, and he nodded.

"That's the only way to do it," he said gravely, then flashed a purely devastating smile, and Christa gladly could have choked him.

He looked across at her and he said, equably, "I hope you're feeling better."

"I wasn't aware I'd been sick," she told him stiffly.

"Honora seemed to think something had upset you," he said. "Let's say, at least, you certainly have upset *her*."

"I'm sorry if that's so," Christa replied, and this, at least, she meant.

"Well," Paul said reasonably, "perhaps you can explain matters to her when we get back."

Christa had never before detested him quite so thoroughly.

She knew that her own eyes were sparking but this, oddly, only seemed to have the effect of diminishing the anger in his, and she caught a gleam of decided amusement and bit her lip to keep from lashing out at him verbally in front of Glenda's mother.

She made herself say quietly, "Glenda has gotten me a job here in Albany, and I'm going to share the apartment her parents have been arranging for her here in the house."

"Darling!" Paul said, managing to put a wealth of endearment into what clearly was a single word of protest.

Mrs. Murray beamed, and Christa had the sharp impression that Glenda's mother was finding this real life drama ever so much more interesting than her daily television stories.

He turned to Mrs. Murray, flashing that smile again, and he was so *damnably* attractive that Christa could hardly blame the older woman for all but melting. The thing was, Christa told herself fiercely, that Mrs. Murray didn't *really* know him!"

He said, deprecatingly, "I didn't want to tell tales out of school, Mrs. Murray," and Christa flinched at his use of such a cliché expression, "but now that Christa's with us I'm going to confess to you that we had a—disagreement over the holidays."

He might as well have said "a lovers' quarrel," and Christa watched, silently wrathful, as Mrs. Murray accepted this with downright relish.

"Christa *is* impetuous," he went on, speaking as if she were a small child not even in the same room with them, "she was even ready to give up her career, which is out of the question."

His cool gray eyes met Christa's deep blue ones as he said this, and she felt a start of real surprise.

This time, he wasn't being artful. He meant it!

Her *career*. The word came ringing about her ears, as Paul continued, seriously, "She probably hasn't said much to you about this, Mrs. Murray, or even to your daughter. But you see, she's going to be making her concert debut in the fall, either at the Kennedy Center of Performing Arts or with the New York Philharmonic, it hasn't definitely been decided yet. In the interim, she is going to have to spend every possible moment studying and practicing."

"How absolutely *wonderful* . . ." Mrs. Murray began, and Paul nodded.

He said, in a tone that was pure steel, although the enchanted Mrs. Murray was quite unaware of this, "Yes. It is, isn't it?"

They started back for Lakeport the following morning, and the fact that the drive all the way was pure torture to Christa had nothing at all to do with the miserable weather.

Paul had acceded to the Murrays' request that he spend the night, in view of the snowstorm, and he had definitely dominated the evening, without in the least seeming to do so.

Mr. Murray immediately had liked him, on a man to man basis, and they found a surprising number of things in common to talk about. Paul could discuss anything from politics to fishing with equal ease, Christa discovered. He was by no means an artist who had been so enmeshed in his work and himself that he knew nothing else, and this multidimensional aspect of him was new to her.

Glenda, returning home, had known instantly who he was, and had become as enraptured with him as her mother was, and Paul had turned on the full chandelier of his charm for both Murray women, while Christa gritted her teeth.

When the two girls got into their respective beds that night, Glenda said, switching out the lamp on the table between them, "How could you *possibly* have walked out on him, Christa?"

Christa was glad that the darkness in the room made it unnecessary for her to try to camouflage the expression on her face!

Once she and Paul were in the Corvette together, however, and the Murrays waved them off, the climate altered.

Paul became considerably colder than the snow outside, and Christa, huddled into the corner of the car, was glad that he evidently had decided to remain silent until they reached Lakeport.

The weather hampered their speed; what might normally have been a four-hour drive stretched into a considerably longer one, and in the early afternoon Paul conceded that they had better stop for lunch.

Facing her across the table in the small pine-paneled restaurant he had chosen, he said bluntly, "You look awful!"

"You always *are* so flattering!" she retorted sweetly.

"I don't feel very much like flattering you at the moment," he told her. "I think you owe me both an apology and an explanation."

She clutched at the first work. "An *apology?*" she demanded incredulously.

"Yes. Ted and Gloria and I got to the house New Year's Day evening to find Honora in an absolute turmoil. It seems she had just received a ridiculous letter from you saying that you were leaving forever, or something equally dramatic."

The muscle in his jaw twitched. "I hardly need tell you that there was also a small envelope for me with the little gold piano I'd given you in it, and some cryptic remark about its current lack of validity. Just what did you mean by *that?*"

He had been suppressing his anger but now it surged forth again, and it would have been easy to be intimidated by the expression in his steely eyes.

But Christa had had her share of being intimidated by him. She had *no* intention of backing down again!

"I think you should *know* what I meant without my having to spell it out," she said, matching his coldness. But as she spoke there was something else clutching at her heart, twisting it with an almost physical force.

He and Ted and *Gloria* had arrived together at the lakeside mansion!

This meant that even now Gloria De Platte was in residence at the Talbot house!

He said, and she knew he was referring to the little gold piano again, "Well, perhaps I'm obtuse, but I'll admit that your returning my Christmas gift in that fashion stung."

She could not resist it. She said, "How do you suppose I felt about what you did with *my* Christmas gift?"

There was chagrin in his smile. "All right," he said. "Touché. But I did apologize."

"And I'm not about to apologize!" Christa told him. "You—you can't simply walk over every woman in your life and always get away with it, Paul."

The eyebrow lifted. "*I* walk over every woman in my life?" he demanded.

"When you wish to. You think you can get away with *anything* because you're handsome and famous and rich . . ."

"I think I've restrained myself from getting away with what I *think* I might have been able to get away with with you, Christa," he told her drily.

She stared at him, infuriated, and he said quickly, "I'm sorry. I shouldn't have said that."

"There are a lot of things you should neither have said nor done," she assured him, trying to blot out the memory of those times when he had kissed her, when they had come so close to making love.

"Last night, as an example, you simply *twisted*

Glenda and her mother into your way of thinking," she accused him, and then a sudden suspicion swirled down upon her.

"How did you know where I was?" she demanded.

"Your friend Glenda phoned Honora yesterday," he said without evasion. "First thing in the morning, as a matter of fact. So, we set off right after breakfast . . ."

"We?"

"I drove Gloria back to New York before coming on to Albany to pick you up."

The stab of relief was painful in itself, but even worse was the knowledge that Glenda had actually *betrayed* her.

"My *friend* Glenda!" she said bitterly.

"She *is* your friend, Christa," Paul said quietly. "Just because you've turned against me for some weird reason don't start turning against everyone else. Glenda phoned Honora because she knew you were miserably unhappy. She's lived with you before, you know, I think without realizing it you gave her a very deep sense then of what music means to you. Glenda is an exceedingly sharp young lady. She told Honora that much as she wanted you to share both a job and her home, she felt it would be a terrible mistake on your part to give up your career."

"My *career!*" she said scornfully. "That word again! I *have* no career!"

His gray eyes were level, and there was neither anger nor mirth in them now.

"That's where you are so wrong," he told her.

Chapter Twelve

It was late afternoon when they arrived in Lakeport, and as they turned in the driveway and Christa saw the huge house looming ahead, every window blazing with lights, she knew a sense of homecoming that refused to be suppressed.

"It looks as if Honora has pulled out all the stops to welcome you back," Paul observed drily.

Honora was waiting in the foyer. She seemed really distraught, clutching Christa as if she could never bear to let her go again.

She said, under her breath, "How *could* you, darling! But we'll talk later about it, privately." And she cast a withering glance at her nephew.

Paul tightened his lips. The implication was clear that it was he who had caused Christa to leave, but he held his tongue. Christa, knowing that Honora, at least, was one person in the world of whom he was genuinely fond, realized that this was a bitter pill for him to swallow.

Ted, hugging her, said, "Why didn't you have a talk with your old Uncle Theodore before you took off?"

There was something rather odd about the way he said this, and Christa looked up at him swiftly. She had the distinct impression that Ted had something significant to tell her, but that, too, would have to come later.

Paul brought the reunion to an end by saying, "I think Christa and I could both use a drink before dinner; something stronger than sherry, tonight. It's been quite a drive."

Fitch, who was hovering around, as was Martha, nodded quickly and said, "I'll bring cocktails to the family room. Martha can hold dinner for half an hour or so, can't you, Martha?"

Martha, too, seemed very much relieved to see her back, and Christa began to feel very humble, thinking how much she had come to mean to Honora and Fitch and Martha and, quite possibly, to Ted as well.

She only wished that she could include Paul in this list, but, she thought bitterly, she had come to represent a property, not a person, to him.

If he was serious about her career, if he really *meant* that bit about her making a concert debut next fall, then he must now visualize himself in the role of a puppet master, she decided. Was she the first of an entire series of students who would become Paul's puppets, she wondered, and knew that she had *no* desire to have her own strings pulled by him.

No, that was not what she wanted from him at all!

He was watching her, she had the disconcerting impression that he literally could read her mind, and this had too much of a "Svengali" touch for comfort.

He said to Honora, "Christa and I will join you in just a moment. But I'd like a private word in the library with her first."

Ted intervened before Honora could protest, which she seemed about to do, and led her gently toward the family room. Paul went over to the library door, but Christa did not make a move toward him. She waited until Ted and Honora were out of sight, and then she said, coldly, "I don't think there's anything 'private' we need to talk about."

"On the contrary," he said, "there is. I've something to show you. Please, Christa, don't make me carry you in there bodily!"

He looked almost as tired as she felt, and yet there was a strength to him, that virility of which she was always so conscious seemed to sweep out toward her, making her even giddier than usual, for she was already both confused and exhausted.

She had not meant to speak the words aloud, but to her horror an epithet came clearly from her lips.

Did he really wince slightly, or was this a mere fancy on her part? Christa wasn't sure, and he said only, almost negligently, "You *do* despise me, don't you!" making it a comment rather than a question.

She did not try to deny it. It was better to have him think she despised him than for him to know the truth of her feelings toward him, she told herself, as she followed him into the library.

He went on ahead to turn on the lights by the desk, and then he said shortly, "Okay. Look for yourself. I asked that no one disturb this while I went to get you, and I see they've followed my wishes."

The huge desk, she saw with astonishment, was covered with sheets of the very same sort of musical composition paper she had bought him for Christmas! With it were pencils and pens and erasers and everything else one could possibly need to write a song, or a sonata—or even a symphony.

"The theme has been going through my head ever since you first put the thought into my mind," he said now, almost reluctantly. "It has gotten to the point where there is no staying it, and I spoke about it the other night to a friend who was a guest at Gloria's party, and is very knowledgeable about such things, and he convinced me that I should not even try to."

He looked directly into her eyes. He said, "I'm going to write a concerto for piano, Christa, and *you* are going to play it! Your debut as a performer and mine as a composer will occur at one and the same concert. So make up your mind to it, your life from this moment on is going to be *all* piano. Honora has agreed. She says the time has come with her book when she needs to start doing her own editing on the manuscript anyway, and when that is through, any good typist can complete the job for her.

"Honora and Ted and I have all agreed that you are to move in here, where you will be able to concentrate on music with nothing else to disturb you. We have approximately nine months to bring you to full form."

He smiled briefly, but there was no mirth in the smile. "It's a rather appropriate gestation period," he commented. "In the meantime, your neighbor, Mr. Anderson, is involved in contracting as well as insurance, though I don't think you knew that. He will take over renovating the music school according to your wishes, but I want you to make your plans with him within the next day or so before we get down to serious work. After that the music school must have only your secondary attention. When you have made your debut, and have some concept of what your future is going to be, you can make your decision regarding what you wish to do with it."

The enormity of what he was saying was too much to grasp, under the circumstances. She felt that she must seem truly stupid as she stood staring at him, unable to find a proper choice of words.

She wanted to pour out a veritable torrent that would be, at least partly, a protest to his high-handedness. She wanted to challenge him for his audacity in thinking that he could simply arrange her life for her without even the courtesy of consultation! Yet she could only gape.

Again, he seemed to read her mind, and his smile was bitter.

"I'm not asking you to do this for *me*, Christa," he said. "I think I know what your answer to that would be! I *am* asking you to do it for Honora. She's quite a marvelous person and she means a great deal to me. Ironically, perhaps, *you* seem to have come to mean even more to her than I do! So at least make me one promise, will you? Don't let her down!''

Life, indeed, became all music. By the time mid-January had arrived, Mr. Anderson had made the arrangements for interior work on the music school, and plans were laid out for painting, come spring, landscaping and a variety of other details that Christa, herself, had not even thought about.

She demurred, at first, at the thought of moving into the lakeside mansion, But Honora convinced her that it was only logical to do so, and this proved to be true.

Paul was more demanding and relentless than ever, as a teacher. There were lessons every morning, followed, always, by at least a brief walk after lunch even when the weather was so icy that Christa thought she would freeze before she could get back into the house.

In the afternoons, she would spend hours at the console of the great piano, practicing and practicing and practicing, while Paul worked alone in the library until, finally, there was enough of his concerto written down for her to begin to study and interpret it.

The day that she played the first movement was unforgettable. The haunting theme recurred again and again, and with it was interwoven a musical fabric that had a strength and power that astonished her, despite the fact that she was the one who initially had suspected he had talent as a composer.

Winter merged into spring, but Christa was so busy at work that she barely noticed the change in seasons. One day she saw forsythia in bloom, and she stood enraptured by its golden radiance.

"Captured sunlight," she said, and Paul, standing

by her side, stirred, and for just a moment she had the feeling that he was going to take her in his arms.

The moment passed, however. There was nothing of the truly personal in their relationship now, he kept it entirely on a teacher-student level when they were alone. When they were with Honora and Ted at dinner, or in the evenings, he treated her as he might a casual friend, or, perhaps, an adolescent niece.

Honora had expressed her opinion of Gloria De Platte volubly, during the first conversation she and Christa had together after Christa's return. It would have been impossible for Honora to be really discourteous to a guest under her own roof, but Christa was certain that Gloria had been given polite but cool treatment by Paul's aunt.

Paul and Gloria still were in frequent communication, at least by phone, Christa knew, for often Fitch came to the family room door, evenings, to announce that Miss De Platte was calling, and Paul always took such calls on the telephone in the library.

Christa wondered if perhaps, with the coming of summer, he might invite Gloria to Lakeport again. In the meantime, Ted was making frequent trips to New York, and inevitably, upon his return, there were long conferences between Paul and himself, these, too, held in the library behind closed doors.

When summer did finally arrive, there was no mention of a possible visit from Gloria, and Christa's own personal horizons did enlarge, to an extent. Paul drove her over to the music school occasionally, and she was delighted with the progress being made. Honora had gotten in on the act, choosing wallpaper patterns and matching paint colors, and she had an excellent eye for decor. She had held to the Victorian, using the old Tiffany lamps and Carnival glass pieces and the other *objets d'art* of that rather stuffy period, sometimes for their vibrant color, sometimes for their curiosity.

As summer deepened, Paul suggested that they swim off the beach in front of the house before lunch each day, foregoing their usual walk, and since Christa didn't possess a bathing suit he drove her into town personally, one day, to get one, and she thought for a moment that he was going to come into the shop with her to help her make a selection.

Instead, he waited in the car, but he did admit his curiosity about her purchase when she came out with a shopping bag in hand. She flushed slightly, for it had been a hard decision. She had never worn anything so revealing as a bikini, and it was the saleslady, actually a girl about her own age, who had insisted that she try one, instead of the relatively drab one-piece suit Christa had pulled off the rack.

Thanks to Martha's good food, she had filled out, and the pale yellow bra top, with what she considered appallingly sketchy pants that tied at each side, revealed what even she had to admit was a great improvement in her figure.

"You look like a movie star in that!" the salesgirl said, and Christa laughed, but then decided to succumb to flattery. After all, why not?

Still, she felt hesitant about producing the suit and showing it to Paul, but he merely laughed.

"Okay," he said. "You can give it its first ducking when we get home."

She was not ready to appear before him in the bikini quite so soon, so she said quickly, "What about my practicing?"

"I'll give you an hour off," he said generously. "We can afford it. You're doing so well I'd say we're definitely ahead of schedule."

After they got back to the house, though, she hesitated for a long while after donning the bikini, before starting out to the lakefront to meet Paul, and then she wrapped herself in a terry robe that went all the way to her ankles, before leaving the house.

With the coming of summer, the pebbles had been

raked off the beachfront for a considerable area, creating a stretch of sand. Paul, she saw now, as she neared it, was lying on a giant beach towel, his eyes closed, and she swallowed hard at the sight of him.

The bright blue bathing trunks he was wearing fit him so snugly that little was left to the imagination about his own, powerful, male physique. Her eyes traveled the length of his long body, coming to linger upon his beloved face, and the generous, sensuous curve of his lips, and she felt as if a fire had suddenly been tingled within her, literally sweeping through her until she wanted him so badly that she nearly cried out.

When she took off her robe, she became aware that he had opened his eyes, and he was staring up at her with a blaze of naked longing stamped clearly upon his own features.

He sprang to his feet in a quick leap, and she saw that revealing jaw muscle tighten and begin to twitch.

He said, "That's *quite* a bathing suit!" And before she could respond he grabbed her hand and was pulling her into the water.

They were both good swimmers, although he consistently outdistanced her, despite her best efforts. Finally they swam out to the float that had been anchored offshore, and he, climbing aboard it ahead of her, reached out a hand to help her up.

This was his good right hand, the fingers strong and firm, and he did not release her once she was up on the boards beside him. His eyes seemed to be devouring the cleavage between her breasts, and now his fingers followed his eyes, finding their way underneath the brief damp bra, feeling both one breast and then the other, while she tried desperately to muster self-control, but he was too much for her.

She could *not* draw away from him, she let him

envelop her with his arms, and she thrust her lips up to meet his. They clung together, not even thinking of the house behind them on top of the rise, and the many, many windows that faced their way.

"Oh, Christa," Paul groaned, "it would take a saint to resist you, and I'm not a saint, nor a monk, even though I've been playing the *part* of a monk for heaven knows how long now. . . ."

His lips descended again, and now his fingers began searching further, but then, before she even knew what was about to happen, he literally pushed her off the raft and he dived in the water beside her. He deliberately splashed water in her face as if she were a child he had been cavorting with, and then he said, "Race you back to the house!" and he was off, swimming shoreward with steady, even strokes.

Christa, humiliated, clung to the raft, watching him as the distance between them widened, and the distance, itself, seemed symbolic to her.

True, she had succeeded in attracting him as a woman, she had aroused him thoroughly, she was well aware of that, but he had aroused her too and, even though knowing it, had literally thrown her away!

She shivered. Paul had the willpower to thrust anything out of his life that did not fit in with his plan of the moment, she decided.

For a moment, she almost felt sorry for Gloria De Platte!

With the approach of fall, the pace quickened. Now Christa was spending a great deal of time with Paul's concerto, until it began to seem to her that she could never again bear to even *hear* the theme that had so entranced her originally, yet alone play it again once the concert was over.

The first colors of autumn brushed the tree leaves, and there began to be endless matters to take under consideration. A dressmaker from New York whom Honora had known for years came for consultation about the gown that would be created for Christa to wear at the concert, and a makeup artist who was famous throughout the musical and theatrical world came for the weekend to make a disconcertingly thorough study of Christa's face, and to suggest the most effective hair style for the evening.

These were but a few of seemingly hundreds of details to be attended to, things that Christa had never given thought to, and she realized fully now that she was in extremely professional hands.

At moments she had the whimsical sensation that she was a race horse being groomed for something like the Kentucky Derby. Would they throw a blanket of roses over her if she managed to make the finish line? she wondered.

As it was, she marveled at her original naiveté; if, in the beginning, she had indeed been a kind of therapeutic tool, used by both Honora and Ted for the sake of giving Paul an interest in life, then this certainly had stopped being true a long, long time ago.

She truly *did* feel now as if she were more property than person, yet there were moments when she was awed by her own talent, when she could not believe that it was she executing passages she would not have believed she ever could master.

Weeks ago, the matter of where she would make her debut had been settled, and she could not quite believe this, either. She was to appear at Lincoln Center, with the New York Philharmonic Symphony Orchestra itself as the "accompanist." She would appear in the second half of the program, playing Paul's concerto.

As October passed, the days became indistinguishable to her, and she fell into bed each night, exhausted. Fabrics had been brought from New York to be examined and rejected by Honora, until finally a length of shimmering champagne brocade proved acceptable; it would catch just enough light to emphasize her slender presence against the ebony of the piano bench and the piano itself, without being dazzling enough to distract from the music.

Honora favored an upswept hair style, definitely more sophisticated, but in this one area Paul firmly countermanded his aunt's wishes. Christa's hair, he said, was to be worn in what was now her usual style; brushed with not much more than a hint of a wave, curling softly about her shoulders.

Honora was more than willing to bedeck her with all sorts of glittering jewels for the occasion, but when Christa produced the antique topaz and gold necklace that had been her Aunt Faith's, Honora had to concede that this was a perfect choice, and should be Christa's only ornament.

She agreed with Honora yet she wished, achingly, that Paul would suggest she wear the little gold piano he had given her at Christmas, which she subsequently had returned to him. She wondered now what he had done with it? Very probably he had consigned it to the fireplace in his anger, just as he had her own Christmas present to him.

She wondered if Ted knew about the small gold piano, but she hesitated to ask him, nor did she have much, if any, time for private conversation with Ted. The night Paul had brought her back to Lakeport Ted had indicated that there was something he wanted to tell her, something, at least, which he wished she had asked *him* about, but whatever this might be remained as much of a mystery now as it had been then.

One day, she awakened to realize that it was precisely a year since she had received the call from the hospital telling her that her Uncle Julian had suffered a heart attack and was asking for her.

In a sense, it seemed like yesterday since that moment when she had first confronted Honora in the hospital lobby. In a sense, it seemed forever.

Luigi Florenso, the conductor of the New York Philharmonic, had been a violinist of world renown himself before he made the decision to devote himself to the podium, where he had, over the past decade, gained an international reputation.

Christa learned, early in the fall, that Paul had been a protégé of Florenso's when he was not much older than she was now, but even so she was staggered when she was told that Florenso was coming to Lakeport for the weekend.

It made her realize even more than she had already how totally her own "career" rested upon Paul's reputation. It would have been unthinkable, under ordinary circumstances, to book an unknown pianist for a major New York performance at which an important new musical composition would be heard for the first time.

It was Florenso who told her quietly, in the brief time they had to themselves before joining the others for drinks, that Paul had insisted she was the only person in the *world* he would permit to play his concerto at its premiere, and the sage conductor admitted that initially he had had his doubts about this.

Since hearing her perform, however, he added quickly, those doubts had been more than resolved!

Christa, puzzled, had wondered if she must be dreaming, for she certainly had never played before Luigi Florenso. But the famous conductor had merely smiled at her bewilderment and said, "It was a tape of your rendition that I heard, of course, my child."

Honora came, just at that moment, to ask them to join the others in the drawing room, and Christa was glad this spared her the necessity of making a reply.

Paul had, to be sure, made no secret of taping some of the lessons from almost the beginning of their time together. His expressed object, though, had been to record her progress, and she deeply resented the fact that he had taped her rendition of his concerto, then, via Ted no doubt, sent it to New York for Florenso to hear, without even mentioning that he was doing so.

Why must he be so high-handed?

She was inwardly annoyed throughout the dinner, and thankful that she was not asked to play afterward. Disciplined though she had become, she was certain that, tonight, her fingers would betray her emotions.

The next morning after breakfast, however, Florenso took her into the drawing room with him, closed all the doors, and then politely asked her to play for him.

He gave no preference, so, with conscious irony, she chose the *Pathétique*. This was the sonata that had, in its way, led Paul to his conclusions about her playing in the first place.

When she had finished, Florenso nodded. "*E ottima!*", he said with satisfaction, then did not exactly please her by adding, "Paul has done very well."

She dreamed, that night, that she was a puppet, and Paul leered above her, jerking the strings that controlled her head and her arms and her legs first one way and then the other, until, finally, she screamed aloud.

She sat up in bed, panting for breath, still gripped by this nightmare vision of his power over her. Then the door to her bedroom opened, she saw the beam of a small pocket flashlight, and realized that Paul, whose room was directly next door to hers, must have heard her cry out.

He asked, urgently, "What is it, Christa? Are you ill?"

She sank back against the pillows, feeling almost afraid of him.

"No," she said, her voice little more than a whisper. "I had a dream. A very bad dream."

He sat down on the side of her bed, switching off the flashlight and pocketing it. He said gently, "Nerves. It happens to everyone, Christa. Perhaps Honora should ask her doctor to prescribe a sedative for you."

"Thank you," she said coldly, "but *I* don't need a placebo."

She could sense his eyes intent on her face, even through the darkness. He sighed, a deep sigh that was singularly expressive. He said, "You think I *did* need one, don't you? You think that's how this whole thing began. Don't deny it, Christa. I've seen the expression in your eyes when you look at me, and it has become increasingly questioning."

"Do you wonder?" she asked sharply.

"No," he said after a moment. "No, I don't. Florenso sensed you were not too pleased at my having sent your tape of the concerto to him. Can't you understand, though, that I owed him at least that much? I realized that I was entirely too close to both my work and to you to be objective about either. . . ."

She wanted to cry out that he was not close to her at all, but he continued, "Looking back over the months I realize what I've demanded of you, Christa, and even as your music has flowered I have seen you shut yourself against me. I've had to harden myself against *you*, but it won't be forever. This final stretch between now and the concert is going to be tense, I don't deny that, but when it is over I will definitely see to it that Ted refuses any bookings offered to you until after the Christmas holidays. In the meantime . . ."

She sat up straight again. "What *about* the meantime?" she demanded. "Are you going to tell me what to do each morning when I wake up, what to wear, how to do my hair, even what to eat? Once the concert is over, are you going to decide just how much freedom I am to be allowed, until the time for another concert is at hand—if, indeed I ever play another concert. Something tells me that one may be enough for the rest of the world, and me too! Are you going to make a decision about whether or not you should make love to me, in my *free time*," she underlined the words scornfully, "just as you've almost done a couple of times before, such as last summer out on the raft . . ."

Her words fell between them like sharp shards of ice. She caught her breath knowing that she was close to the brink of tears, and wishing fervently that he would turn toward her and take her in his arms, and kiss away all the personal demons that seemed to be assailing her.

Instead, he turned away from her, and the silence that developed between them became a long one.

Finally he stood and walked to the window, his back to her. Moonlight shone through the panes, touching his silhouette with silver, highlighting it. The effect was one of terrible loneliness.

Christa saw him raise his right arm and wearily brush his forehead, and at the same time a ray of moonlight brushed his crippled left hand with quick-silver, and she felt a pang of pure shame.

For weeks, in fact for months, she had given no thought at all to Paul's affliction. True, he had made it tremendously clear long since that he did not want pity, but she had not even given him understanding. She had not so much as given a thought to his own sacrifice, and how terribly it must hurt, at moments, to know that he would never be able to play his concerto himself. . . .

"Paul," she began, and the moonlight itself seemed to waver as he shook his head.

"Don't apologize, Christa," he said wearily.

"We've both apologized often enough, and it would be a sham anyway for you to retract a word of what you've just said. I can only tell you that after the concert your free time, *all* your time, your entire *future,* will be *yours,* to do what you want with it."

He was in shadow as he walked across to the bedroom door, turning as he reached the threshold.

"There's no reason for you to harbor any false ideas about gratitude, Christa," he told her, his voice bitter, "because you don't owe me a thing. Don't let anyone try to convince you otherwise. You don't owe me a single, damned thing!"

Chapter Thirteen

The day of the concert Christa learned what the words "stage fright" really meant. She felt like a tightly strung harp, and she was familiar enough with harps to know that the strings upon which one played the high notes were especially fragile, and thus easily snapped.

When the moment came to walk out on stage, was she going to turn to jelly? she wondered. Could she *possibly* sit down at that piano and start to play, once Florenso raised his baton, even though she had been rehearsing with the orchestra for days now, and almost felt as if the musicians were members of her family.

They had been wonderfully warm and encouraging to this newcomer who felt singularly gauche, and, now that the moment was so near at hand, close to terrified.

Yesterday, Florenso had asked her to have a glass of wine with him after rehearsal, and over it he had confided to her that there was one thing about Paul's concerto with which he was not satisfied.

"It is the ending," he said, shaking his head dolefully. "It is such a sad ending. To me it seems that the final crescendo should sound a note of victory, triumph. Instead it leaves a feeling of doom, and I personally do not find this consistent. But then," he added, with an expressive shrug, "one cannot argue with the composer."

The ending of the concerto always *had* bothered Christa, and this she confessed now to Florenso, adding that she had, however, been unable to pinpoint the reasons for her feeling about it as she did.

"I suppose," she said, "that I've been too close to it."

"And too close to Paul?" Florenso suggested.

"No," Christa said, her face revealing more than she realized. "Paul and I are not really close at all."

The conductor smiled, shaking his head. "Ah, little one, little one," he cautioned her, "take care! Even as you start upon what I think will be a great career, do not make a tragic mistake."

They were interrupted by Florenso's concert master who had a problem that needed resolution, but Christa left with the feeling that even had this not happened Florenso would not have elaborated. Thus, his cryptic statement had only added to the conflicting sensations and emotions and uncertainties that seemed to occupy her entire life at the moment, and self-doubt came to take its place with all these other negatives as the time came to dress for the performance.

She told Honora, unhappily, that she was certain she was going to go all to pieces and make a fool of herself.

Honora only smiled and patted her head. "I've been through it a thousand times, darling," she said. "You'll be a wreck until the moment you start to play. Then you'll be all right."

This Christa doubted very much.

She and Honora were staying at Paul's Central Park West apartment, with both Martha and Fitch in attendance, while Paul and Ted were using an apartment a block or so away that belonged to a friend currently in Europe.

Now, as both Martha and Honora hovered over her, making certain that every last detail of her appearance was perfect, she realized that they were only minutes away from leaving for the concert hall, and she had not seen Paul at all.

Ted had stopped by earlier to wish her luck, bestowing a firm kiss upon her before he left. Martha and Fitch, as well as Honora, would be attending the concert. But there was no word at all from Paul, not so much as a phone call, and even though they had had little to say to each other since the night she had had the nightmare, this seemed inexcusable.

She wanted to ask Honora where Paul was, but she was too stubborn to do so. Finally she swept out of the apartment and stood in the elevator, stiff as a waxen doll, climbing into the taxi that waited at the apartment house entrance with the strange, faraway feeling that this was happening to someone else, and that the "real" Christa Emery had been whisked away and was in hiding somewhere.

Florenso was waiting to greet her at the concert hall, and her dressing room was already laden with bouquets of flowers.

Honora and Martha fussed over last-minute touches to her hair and makeup while, on stage, the Philharmonic was now performing the César Franck symphony in D minor, first on the program.

Finally, she heard applause; she knew it was intermission time, and she told herself that *surely* Paul would come in now, to wish her luck for both his sake and hers. But, instead, Honora rose and said, "Darling, I'm going to join the others. We'll be in the first box to the right of the stage, and you may be sure that all of my hopes and prayers will be with you every second."

She hesitated. "Paul asked me to give you this," she said, and she held out a small, rumpled, very familiar looking envelope.

Christa's fingers trembled as she opened it, turning the contents out into her palm.

The little gold piano glinted up at her, and she told herself fiercely that she must not cry. She would ruin her makeup if she cried, she would ruin *everything* if her fingers didn't stop shaking.

Then she saw the small folded note, and she opened it to read: "I know you planned to wear a family heirloom tonight—but I admit this has a special relevance to me. Your own feelings about it must, of course, dictate your decision."

He had not signed the note, but then, Christa acknowledged, there was no need to. It could not possibly have been from anyone else.

She stood in the wings for a final moment that would forever symbolize eternity, and then she was slowly walking across the stage, feeling as if she were carved of pure ice, and the audience began to clap at her appearance.

She turned to face them, and was appalled at their numbers. She was looking out over a veritable sea of faces, for every seat in the house had been taken.

She bowed, exactly as Florenso had coached her to bow, then as she raised her head again she cast a covert glance toward the first box on the right, and wished, violently, that she had not looked.

The impression, brief though the glimpse had been, was indelible. Honora, Ted and Paul were sitting in a row—Martha and Fitch must have been given seats elsewhere, she realized—and next to Paul there was a beautiful brunette in a blazing red dress whom Christa recognized at once from the many newspaper and magazine photos she had seen of her.

Paul had brought Gloria De Platte to the concert where his concerto would be heard for the first time! Did this mean that they would be announcing their wedding date after the concert? Was this the way

what was supposed to be her own night of triumph
was going to be climaxed? Christa wondered, and
was sick at heart at the thought.

She hesitated before taking her seat at the piano,
aware of Florenso's sharp glance. The conductor was
extremely sensitive to the feelings of the artists he
worked with, and Christa had the strong impression
that he knew quite well what was wrong with her.

She looked across at him, meeting his very dark,
almost black eyes. They seemed to shout the message that she *must go on*—but with the message
there also came a kind of gift, an almost tangible
outflow of Florenso's own confidence in her, and she
was bolstered by it.

She took her place at the keyboard, Florenso
lifted his baton, and softly, the orchestra began to
play the first measures of the concerto. Then it came
time for *her* part to begin, and as Christa's fingers
touched the keys in the opening chord she knew that
Honora had been right. It was if nothing else in life
existed. All her concentration, her training, her
talent—and her heart as well—poured out into her
rendition of Paul's music.

She could sense the orchestra's response to her
own brand of magic; violins soared, a harp *arpeggio*
punctuated the end of a measure; she heard the
deep-throated throbbing of the cellos and the beautiful, mellow tones of the oboe, and then she was
coming into her own final solo, approaching that
moment when she would reach the last crescendo,
and in that ultimate moment it was as if the concerto
assumed a life of its own, transcending the music the
way Paul had written it.

She plunged, raising the final crescendo to a
pinnacle of pure victory that resounded throughout
the concert hall, so that when she dropped her hands
and sat back, the audience began to applaud with
wild enthusiasm.

She was called to center stage to take bow after

bow, someone thrust a sheath of red roses into her arms and she forced herself to smile and smile and smile, knowing only too well that the standing ovation being given her was in no way for herself alone. . . .

She kept her eyes averted from the box where Paul was sitting with Gloria De Platte, then finally Florenso led her from the stage for the last time, and she was ushered hastily into her dressing room. Here, Florenso warned her, she could expect only a brief interlude of peace before she must face the usual backstage reception, where the musical elite, as well as all the major critics, would be greeting her. Later, he added, there was to be a party in her honor in the penthouse apartment of some very influential people, where she would be meeting a number of other important people.

"Exhausting," the conductor admitted, "but it is necessary for tonight, *bella*. May I add that your playing was exalted, and your rendition of that last crescendo all I could ever wish for!"

He bent and kissed her hand. He said, "I shall try to ward the hordes off, until you have a moment in which to compose yourself. So take good advantage of it."

Christa nodded, but she was not to have so much as a moment of tranquility. Before she could even sit down there was a brief knock, and Paul came into the room without even waiting to be invited, almost slamming the door behind him.

She drew back at his expression. His face was ashen, his gray eyes glittering, and there was a taut line to his lips.

He stood, glaring down at her, his voice thick with anger. "Just what *did* you think you were doing?" he demanded. As she stared at him blankly, he continued, "Come on, Christa, you know what I'm talking about! What made *you* think you had the right to change my ending!"

The contempt in his tone was withering, and so undeserved in view of the audience response the concerto had engendered that she simply could not answer him, which only served to increase his fury.

He grasped her shoulders, the bruising strength of his right hand more than making up for the weakness of his left one so that she winced from the pressure of his fingers.

He said, almost shaking her, "Speak to me! Why did you do it?"

She swallowed hard. She started to say, "Because you . . ." but she was not to be permitted to finish her explanation.

There was another knock at the door and she heard Honora calling her name, and Paul, with a muttered oath, let go of her and swung the door open so suddenly that Honora stepped backward, gazing at him in consternation.

"What is the *matter* with you?" she demanded.

"You might ask Christa that," he growled.

"This isn't the moment for your temperament, Paul," his aunt told him icily. "There are any number of people waiting to greet you and Christa. I'd suggest you both alter the expressions on your faces and come along together."

Honora frowned at both of them. "Smile!" she commanded.

Paul at Christa's side, said under his breath, "Well, this is the first thing you'll have to learn to do, my lovely. Paint a smile on your face and keep it there no matter how you may be feeling inside. . . ."

Then his eyes fell to her throat, and he stopped, even as he was in the process of taking her arm and ushering her out of the dressing room.

She held her breath as he touched the little gold piano, as if to make sure that it really was there.

He said, "I *thought* I saw it when you came on

stage, but I couldn't be entirely sure from that distance. So you *did* wear it, after all. . . ."

There were so many people, all of them gracious, all of them complimentary. Christa shook endless hands, and was graceful in her thanks, and kept her smile painted firmly in place, as they moved on from the concert hall to the party in a penthouse on Beekman Place, high over the East River, where she mingled with people whose names were internationally famous in the world of music and the arts.

She was thoroughly exhausted, but still she kept on going, kept on smiling, she even managed to smile and be gracious when she was introduced to Gloria De Platte, who was even more beautiful than she had seemed from a distance, and whose newspaper pictures surely did not do her justice.

Gloria, in turn, was so charming that it was almost sickening, but managed to make it clear, at the same time, that she did not feel threatened by Paul's pupil. Whenever she was with Paul, she clung to him possessively. She had staked her claim, no doubt about it; what she didn't know was that Christa, long since, had realized this.

Christa was visibly surprised, therefore, when she felt a hand upon her arm as she was striving to keep the painted smile on straight while she made conversation with several admiring strangers, and Paul said, firmly, "Excuse us, will you please?"

Before she realized what was happening he was taking her out into the vestibule, where a smiling maid held out the lovely amber velvet cape Honora had insisted that Christa wear tonight, Paul evidently having made prior arrangements to have it brought to her now.

He literally whisked her into the waiting elevator, and there was a taxi in front of the entrance, too, obviously prearranged.

As they pulled away from the curb, Christa said,

exasperated, "I didn't even have the chance to thank my hosts. . . ."

"One often doesn't," Paul said cryptically, "unless you're willing to keep on going past the saturation point, and I personally have always felt that enough is enough! Honora and Ted assured me that they have enough stamina to hold the fort for us for at least another hour, and you can call your hosts tomorrow or even write them a note, which I'm sure they would always cherish!"

She was too weary to respond.

At the Central Park West apartment, Paul opened the door with his own key and said, "I told Martha and Fitch to go along to bed, I think they're even more worn out than the rest of us. Did you see Glenda and the Murrays backstage, incidentally?"

She had, though it had been impossible to do more than hug Glenda, who kept saying that she "couldn't believe" it, and to promise to come and spend a weekend in Albany as soon as possible.

She said, now, "Yes, and Glenda told me you sent them the tickets. That was very nice of you."

He had taken the velvet cape from her shoulders, and was placing it on a chair, and he paused to glance across at her.

"Well," he said, and she knew without even looking at him that one ironic eyebrow would be raised, "that's the first *decent* thing you've said to me within recent memory."

Fitch had left lights on in the living room, and now Paul, walking ahead of her, flung himself down on a couch, ran a hand through his thick, dark hair, ruffling it, then took off the stiffly formal bow tie he had been wearing and tossed it on the nearby coffee table.

A moment later, he unfastened the top two buttons on his shirt, and he grinned at her as he did so.

"Don't you even feel like kicking off your shoes?" he asked her, then added, almost wistfully, "when I first met you again, I seem to remember that you weren't wearing any shoes at all."

When I first met you again . . .

He sobered, and his eyes seemed to darken. He said, quietly, "You know, without my adding to all the verbal bouquets, that you were superb tonight, Christa. Ted is going to have a hard time keeping you from another concert booking until you tell him you're ready for a commitment. . . ."

"Until *I* tell him."

"Yes. I told you once this concert was over you would be mistress of your own destiny. I shan't be making any more of your decisions, Christa. I was certainly never cut out to be anybody's manager. Ted, however, will do an excellent job for you."

"And you?" She could not refrain from asking the question.

"What about me?"

"Will you be getting married soon?" She did not realize how small her voice sounded.

"Me?" He frowned up at her quizzically. "I should rather doubt it."

"Does Miss De Platte favor such a long engagement?"

"I wouldn't know what kind of engagement Gloria favors."

"How could you help but know?" Now Christa did kick off her shoes, and she sat down in an armchair opposite him. "She's been your fiancée for the past two years—or is it even longer?"

Paul raised that eternally ironic eyebrow and asked, a hint of amusement in his voice, "What *is* this? Gloria has never been my fiancée for two seconds, let alone two years!"

Christa had the sudden feeling that this was what Ted had been trying to tell her for quite some time now, yet had never managed to do so. Still . . .

"It was in the paper," she persisted. "I have a clipping . . ."

He seemed honestly astonished. "You have a clipping about Gloria and me?"

"I have a whole box of clippings about you," she faltered.

A strange expression crossed his face. "Dating back to the days when you were hero worshipping?" he suggested.

"I—I suppose you might call it that."

"But then, when you really got to know me, you found out there was truth to the old cliché about idols having clay feet, didn't you?"

"No," Christa said stubbornly.

"Would you repeat that, please?"

"I said no," Christa repeated. She took the plunge. "If she isn't your fiancée, why did you ask her to sit in the box with you tonight?"

"Ah," he said, "so you *did* notice! Well, as it happens, I didn't ask her, she invited herself. Her parents also have a box—season tickets—and she went to the concert with them. However, she opted to join us, and since there was a vacant chair right next to me I could hardly refuse her. We *are* old friends. . . ."

"You brought her to Lakeport last New Year's," Christa said.

"Yes. I brought her along because I was stupid enough to think the two of you might be friends, and that she might be helpful to you."

Something sparked in his eyes. He said, disbelievingly, "Christa, are you trying to tell me that you left Lakeport because . . ."

She nodded before he even finished. She said, her voice smaller than ever, "Yes."

"Because you thought that *Gloria* . . ."

"Please," she said miserably. "Please, let's not go into it!"

"Very well," Paul agreed, "I'll admit that there are more important things to go into—like what you did to the ending of the concerto tonight, although after I talked to Florenso I realized it wasn't entirely your doing. He admitted he told you he wasn't happy with the original ending."

"Nor was I," Christa said steadily.

"Can you tell me why?"

She swallowed hard. "Because you deserve victory, not defeat," she said. "Even at that, you weren't ready to accept the victory though, were you? I heard those cries out in the concert hall for the composer. They wanted you to come up and take your bow on the stage too, but Florenso told me you'd already informed him that you wouldn't, under any circumstances. . . ."

"Tonight was *yours*," he said, and there was no smile on his face now. "This was your victory, Christa. No one else deserved to share it."

"On the contrary," she said, "tonight was really yours and it was you who deserved that applause. We both know that but for you and your concerto I would never have been there at all. And as for your having clay feet—well, nothing could be further from the truth than that. My talent will never match yours, and don't shake your head, because it is true. You know it in your heart and so do I, and I don't resent it. But, now that I've had a taste of—of what it's like out there, and even more especially since I've come to know what the piano really means to me, I would say that far from being an idol with clay feet you're the bravest person I've ever met."

He was staring at her incredulously, and the look on his face made her want to cry.

She said, unsteadily. "Paul—if, after tonight, you're going to simply turn me over to Ted, I . . ."

"Yes?"

"I don't want to go on with it!"

She stood and made her way almost blindly to the window, blinking back tears as she stared out over the vast expanse of Central Park, crisscrossed with light patterns that were like pearl and rhinestone necklaces, studded, here and there, with the vivid ruby or emerald of a flashing traffic light.

She felt Paul close beside her, she could smell the provocative scent of the shaving lotion he used, and now he clasped his arms around her waist, drawing her toward him.

He said, "Can you possibly be saying what I think you're saying? Can you possibly be trying to tell me that . . ."

He seemed almost afraid to continue, and she gently finished the question for him. "That I love you?" she asked. "Oh, darling, I've loved you for such a long, long time. But I thought you saw in me only ten fingers that could, perhaps, perform on a keyboard. . . ."

"A surrogate talent?"

"I suppose you'd call it that. Honora and Ted both seemed to feel that you needed an incentive when you first came back to Lakeport, and that I would be a kind of therapy for you. You, yourself, seemed to confirm this in everything you did and said. Increasingly, I came to feel that you saw me as a puppet, not a person."

"A puppet that I, of course, was manipulating?"

"Well—yes," she confessed.

"I thought," he said in turn, "that you saw me only as someone who long ago had become a symbol to you. I thought you saw in me only the concert pianist, not the man, and then—well, you have a very revealing face, my darling. Sometimes it virtually cried out your pity for me. I became terribly afraid that you would confuse pity with love, especially at those times when I couldn't keep myself from kissing you, and you responded. . . ." His laugh was wry. He said, "I admit that in the beginning I thought up the idea of the lessons for an ulterior motive. I did realize you had talent, I discovered that standing outside your studio window in the cold and listening to you play. But I have to admit I didn't know how *much* talent you had until we started working together."

"Then why did you want to teach me?" she asked.

"Because it was the only way I could be sure of keeping you near me," he said simply. "I felt if we were together on a daily basis, just maybe I could convince you to learn to love me. But, as time went on and we became more deeply involved, everything seemed to be going the other way. . . ."

Christa no longer hesitated. She reached up to encircle Paul with her arms, tilting his head down until she could kiss him, freely, completely, entirely of her own volition.

His quick response was so total, so ardent, that everything else that had happened tonight paled before its radiance.

As he held her to him, he said, "It's a good thing Honora and Ted will be arriving here any second, for I couldn't possibly make any guarantees about my behavior. As it is, let there be no more concerts until after our wedding, is that agreed?"

"No," she said, and as he drew back, frowning down on her, she added, lightly but firmly, "there will be no more concerts until after our very long honeymoon!"

6 brand new Silhouette Special Editions yours for 15 days–Free!

For the reader who wants more...more story...more detail and description...more realism...and more romance...in paperback originals, 1/3 longer than our regular Silhouette Romances. Love lingers longer in new Silhouette Special Editions. Love weaves an intricate, provocative path in a third more pages than you have just enjoyed. It is love as you have always wanted it to be—and more —intriguingly depicted by your favorite Silhouette authors in the inimitable Silhouette style.

15-Day Free Trial Offer

We will send you 6 new Silhouette Special Editions to keep for 15 days absolutely free! If you decide not to keep them, send them back to us, you pay nothing. But if you enjoy them as much as we think you will, keep them and pay the invoice enclosed with your trial shipment. You will then automatically become a member of the Special Edition Book Club and receive 6 more romances every month. There is no minimum number of books to buy and you can cancel at any time.

Silhouette Romance

IT'S YOUR OWN SPECIAL TIME

Contemporary romances for today's women.
Each month, six very special love stories will be yours
from SILHOUETTE. Look for them wherever books are sold
or order now from the coupon below.

$1.50 each

Hampson	☐ 1 ☐ 4 ☐ 16 ☐ 27	Browning	☐ 12 ☐ 38 ☐ 53 ☐ 73
	☐ 28 ☐ 40 ☐ 52 ☐ 64 ☐ 94		☐ 93
Stanford	☐ 6 ☐ 25 ☐ 35 ☐ 46	Michaels	☐ 15 ☐ 32 ☐ 61 ☐ 87
	☐ 58 ☐ 88	John	☐ 17 ☐ 34 ☐ 57 ☐ 85
Hastings	☐ 13 ☐ 26 ☐ 44 ☐ 67	Beckman	☐ 8 ☐ 37 ☐ 54 ☐ 72
Vitek	☐ 33 ☐ 47 ☐ 66 ☐ 84		☐ 96

$1.50 each

☐ 3 Powers	☐ 29 Wildman	☐ 56 Trent	☐ 79 Halldorson
☐ 5 Goforth	☐ 30 Dixon	☐ 59 Vernon	☐ 80 Stephens
☐ 7 Lewis	☐ 31 Halldorson	☐ 60 Hill	☐ 81 Roberts
☐ 9 Wilson	☐ 36 McKay	☐ 62 Hallston	☐ 82 Dailey
☐ 10 Caine	☐ 39 Sinclair	☐ 63 Brent	☐ 83 Hallston
☐ 11 Vernon	☐ 41 Owen	☐ 69 St. George	☐ 86 Adams
☐ 14 Oliver	☐ 42 Powers	☐ 70 Afton Bonds	☐ 89 James
☐ 19 Thornton	☐ 43 Robb	☐ 71 Ripy	☐ 90 Major
☐ 20 Fulford	☐ 45 Carroll	☐ 74 Trent	☐ 92 McKay
☐ 21 Richards	☐ 48 Wildman	☐ 75 Carroll	☐ 95 Wisdom
☐ 22 Stephens	☐ 49 Wisdom	☐ 76 Hardy	☐ 97 Clay
☐ 23 Edwards	☐ 50 Scott	☐ 77 Cork	☐ 98 St. George
☐ 24 Healy	☐ 55 Ladame	☐ 78 Oliver	☐ 99 Camp

$1.75 each

☐ 100 Stanford	☐ 105 Eden	☐ 110 Trent	☐ 115 John
☐ 101 Hardy	☐ 106 Dailey	☐ 111 South	☐ 116 Lindley
☐ 102 Hastings	☐ 107 Bright	☐ 112 Stanford	☐ 117 Scott
☐ 103 Cork	☐ 108 Hampson	☐ 113 Browning	☐ 118 Dailey
☐ 104 Vitek	☐ 109 Vernon	☐ 114 Michaels	☐ 119 Hampson

Silhouette Romance

15-Day Free Trial Offer
6 Silhouette Romances

6 Silhouette Romances, free for 15 days! We'll send you 6 new Silhouette Romances to keep for 15 days, absolutely free! If you decide not to keep them, send them back to us. You pay nothing.

Free Home Delivery. But if you enjoy them as much as we think you will, keep them by paying the invoice enclosed with your free trial shipment. We'll pay all shipping and handling charges. You get the convenience of Home Delivery and we pay the postage and handling charge each month.

Don't miss a copy. The Silhouette Book Club is the way to make sure you'll be able to receive every new romance we publish before they're sold out. There is no minimum number of books to buy and you can cancel at any time.

This offer expires July 31, 1982